Charles L. Harris

THE MASTER KEY

Rob was surrounded by a group of natives

THE MASTER KEY

An Electrical Fairy Tale

FOUNDED UPON THE MYSTERIES OF ELECTRICITY
AND THE OPTIMISM OF ITS DEVOTEES. IT WAS
WRITTEN FOR BOYS, BUT OTHERS MAY READ IT

BY

L. FRANK BAUM

ILLUSTRATIONS BY

F. Y. CORY

WITH A NEW INTRODUCTION BY
DONALD L. GREENE
AND
DOUGLAS G. GREENE

HYPERION PRESS, INC.
WESTPORT, CONNECTICUT

Library of Congress Cataloging in Publication Data

Baum, Lyman Frank, 1856–1919.
  The master key.

  SUMMARY: A young boy accidentally summons the
Demon of Electricity who gives him certain electrical
gifts to show the world.
  Reprint of the 1901 ed. published by Bowen–Merrill,
Indianapolis.
  [1. Fantasy. 2. Electricity—Fiction]
I. Cory, Fanny Y., illus. II. Title.
PZ7.B327Mal5   [Fic]   73-13247
ISBN 0–88355–103–9
ISBN 0–88355–132–2 (pbk.)

Published in 1901
by the Bowen-Merrill Company, Indianapolis
Copyright 1901
by The Bowen-Merrill Company

Copyright © 1974 by Hyperion Press, Inc.

Hyperion reprint edition 1974

Library of Congress Catalogue Number 73-13247

ISBN 0-88355-103-9 (cloth ed.)
ISBN 0-88355-132-2 (paper ed.)

Printed in the United States of America

To my son

ROBERT STANTON BAUM

L. FRANK BAUM:
From Oz to Science Fiction

By David L. Greene and
Douglas G. Greene*

L. Frank Baum (1856-1919) is probably America's most important writer of fairy tales for children. Including his collections of short stories, he wrote about thirty fantasy books, and he maintained a high standard in almost all of them. Unfortunately, his greatest and most complex fairy tale, *The Wonderful Wizard of Oz* (1900), has overshadowed his other books, relegating many of them to undeserved obscurity.

In 1901, the year after the *Wizard* appeared, Baum published three fantasies that are very different from each other. *Dot and Tot of Merryland*, like the *Wizard*, is set in an imaginary country. It is hardly surprising that the stories in *American Fairy Tales* have, for the most part, American settings, a considerable departure for fantasies of the time. This collection is ostensibly for children, but the humor in several of the stories is directed at sophisticated and cynical adults. Most daring of all is *The Master Key*, Baum's only successful attempt to write in the genre that has since been named science fiction. This story, "founded upon the mysteries of electricity and the optimism of its devotees," sold well. It went through at least two printings and probably three during its first two years, and Baum remarked that he should not have closed the door on a possible sequel.

The book was published by the Bowen-Merrill Company of Indianapolis at a list price of $1.20. Bowen-Merrill changed its name to Bobbs-Merrill in 1903. Except for distributing the original text sheets in a new binding, Bobbs-

*The authors of this introduction, both Baum enthusiasts, are longtime members of the International Wizard of Oz Society. David L. Greene was editor of *The Baum Bugle*, the Society's official publication; he is also a member of the English Department at Piedmont College in Demorest, Georgia. Douglas G. Greene teaches history at Old Dominion University in Norfolk, Virginia.

Merrill neglected *The Master Key*. No copies have been seen with the Bobbs-Merrill imprint on the title page, although almost all of Baum's other early fantasies were reprinted by that firm in the early 1920s. Possibly the book seemed dated by then, with its references to the Boer War, the German Empire, King Edward VII of Great Britain (who died in 1910), and Émile Loubet who ceased being President of France in 1906. Certainly electricity appeared less a miracle than it had in 1901. What was old-fashioned in 1920 gives *The Master Key* the charm of a period piece today. The novel has not been reprinted for at least seventy years, a situation now remedied by Hyperion Press.

At least part of the initial success of the book was due to the excellent pictures by Fanny Y. Cory. Miss Cory, who was 23 or 24 when the book was published, had already illustrated Baum's short story "The Bad Man" (*The Home Magazine*, February 1901) and would illustrate his fairy tale *The Enchanted Island of Yew* (1903). She was one of the few women regularly illustrating books for children, and within a few years she would become one of the most sought-after illustrators in the country; many of her drawings appeared in *St. Nicholas*, surely the finest children's magazine ever published in America. Her serpentine, *art nouveau* line work and her sturdy use of color* combined to make *The Master Key* an attractive book, and most of the early reviews praised her work. After her association with Baum, she continued illustrating books and later drew several syndicated newspaper cartoons. Her two most popular series, *Sonnysayings* and *Little Miss Muffet* (a competitor of *Little Orphan Annie*), were distributed by King Features Syndicate until she retired in 1956. She died at the age of 94 in 1972.[1]

Whether Baum was consciously imitating early science fiction writers is not known, but his reference in Chapter Two to "great novelists who have written about Martians and their wonderful civilization" indicates that

---

* Unfortunately, excessively high costs prevented the publishers in this reprint edition from reproducing the Cory illustrations in their original color.

[1] Surprisingly little has been published about Miss Cory. The most complete account is Douglas G. Greene, "Fanny Y. Cory," *The Baum Bugle*, XVII (Spring 1973), 17 - 20, which includes a brief bibliography. The *Bugle* is the journal of The International Wizard of Oz Club (220 North Eleventh Street, Escanaba, Michigan 49829).

he was aware of such literature. The immediate inspiration for *The Master Key* was the hobby of his son Robert Stanton Baum, who was fifteen when the book appeared. The early pages of the book contain a slightly exaggerated account of Robert's electrical devices. In his autobiography written in the 1930s (printed in *The Baum Bugle*, Christmas 1970 and Spring 1971), Robert recalled that "I bored holes all through the house and installed wires to operate my various gadgets. For instance, when I wanted privacy in my room, I got it by the very simple expedient of installing a wire from a spark coil and battery to the inside handle of my door. When anyone from the outside took hold of the handle and turned it, contact was made and caused him to change his mind about entering. I also rigged up an apparatus which I attached to our gas lights so that by pushing a button the gas was turned on, and an electric spark ignited it. . . . I rigged up an annunciator drop in the kitchen. . . As soon as I got out of bed, I pushed a button in my room and the annunciator came down with a sign saying, 'start breakfast.' This was the signal to our cook, and by the time I got down, my breakfast was ready. I had various other gadgets strewn all over the house. . . ."

It is easy to imagine Baum looking at his son's workshop and wondering what would happen if all the wires were hooked together haphazardly. Chance experimentation could lead to disaster (*i. e.*, an explosion) or to a major discovery, symbolized by the Demon of Electricity. That these were Baum's thoughts is indicated by his inscription in Robert's copy of the book: "his workshop first gave me the idea of an electrical story and 'The Electrical Demon' was a natural sequence" (quoted by Russell P. MacFall in *To Please A Child, a Biography of L. Frank Baum* Chicago, 1961).

The Joslyn family is in some respects a fictional version of Baum's own family. Rob, the hero of *The Master Key*, is clearly based on his son, Robert Stanton Baum, and Fanny Cory probably used his photograph when she drew the hero of the book. Mr. Joslyn is an idealized version of Baum himself, who must have enjoyed describing Mr. Joslyn as speaking "sagely." ("Joslyn" was the maiden name of Baum's mother-in-law, the suffrage leader

Matilda Joslyn Gage.) Baum had always wanted to have a daughter; the heroines of his Oz books — Dorothy, Ozma, Trot, Betsy Bobbin — are all expressions of this desire. Baum had only sons, so it is not surprising that when he wrote of the Joslyn family he included several daughters.

In 1901, Baum was still a novice at constructing plots. *Dot and Tot of Merryland*, for all its charm, is at best rambling. *The Master Key* is considerably better in its individual episodes than in its overall plot. Though there is a pattern to the novel, it comes close to being a collection of short stories tied together by the motif of the possibilities and dangers of electrical discoveries. Many of the sections are quite good, but others are damaged by the fact that Rob is seldom in real danger. In the last portion of the book he is invulnerable, and earlier he is usually rescued by a *deus ex electrica*. Rob himself was dissatisfied with that situation. He had, as Baum tells us, "a disposition to battle openly with the world and take his chances equally with his fellows, rather than be placed in such an exclusive position that no one could hope successfully to oppose him."

Many of the devices in *The Master Key* are extremely interesting, and Baum used them in some of his later stories. The food tablets reappear in the Oz books as Professor Wogglebug's Square Meal Tablets, and the idea of a magical cloak is used again in *Queen Zixi of Ix* (1905), one of Baum's finest fantasies. The "electric tube," renamed the "electrite," is one of the mechanical contrivances in Baum's pseudonymous *The Boy Fortune Hunters in Yucatan* (1910), a work that has some claim to being science fiction. The "Automatic Record of Events" is a cousin of both Glinda's "Great Book of Records" and Ozma's Magic Picture in the Oz books. Finally, Baum used magical — or at least supernormal — means of flight in many of his books. These include the Gump of *The Marvelous Land of Oz* (1904), the magic wash tub of *The Lost Princess of Oz* (1917), and Glinda's aerial chariot, but the closest parallel to Rob's traveling machine is Button-Bright's flying umbrella in *Sky Island* (1912).

At the beginning of the story Rob resembles the stock hero of the innumerable boy's adventure series of the early part of this century, but he shortly gains in complexity. The Master Key is a novel of education; through experience Rob gains knowledge of himself and of the world. After Rob summons by chance the Demon of Electricity (who is much like the genie of Aladdin's lamp), he is given certain electrical gifts to show to the world. There is never any real suggestion that the gifts are magical, for their properties can be analyzed and duplicated by competent scientists.

As the Demon never tires of saying, Rob is the wrong person to intrust with this task. In Baum's words,

He is, in truth, a typical American boy, possessing an average intelligence not yet regulated by the balance-wheel of experience. The mysteries of electricity were so attractive to his eager nature that he had devoted considerable time and some study to electrical experiment; but his study was the superficial kind that seeks to master only such details as may be required at the moment. Moreover, he was full of boyish recklessness and irresponsibility and therefore difficult to impress with the dignity of science and the gravity of human existence.

It is not surprising that the first of his journeys has little result except to demonstrate his (and, it must be admitted, the author's) chauvinistic attitudes. He visits Boston, a cannibal island, and a pirate ship, before he manages to return home by means of his damaged traveling machine. Instead of taking his devices to scientists to be analyzed, he has merely wished "to astonish the natives."

But the first journey is not entirely futile. Experience of any sort can deepen character, and now Rob's self-confidence is no longer overweening. Before he leaves on his second journey he shows new wisdom by resisting the temptation to look at his family with his "Character Marker." (It should be noted in passing that the idea of the "Character Marker" itself is somewhat facile; seldom can any man's character be categorized as simply and dogmatically as does this device.)

On this journey, Rob's wisdom steadily increases. He is able to help the King of England and the President of France against Graustarkian plots. When he erroneously arrives near the city of Yarkand in China where the Mongols and Turks are battling, he eventually realizes that the war itself is useless. Rob's most impressive act on this journey is to save the two shipwrecked sailors; his erstwhile desire to astonish the natives now seems to the reader a part of the distant past.

Rob faces different types of villains in the first and second journeys. Cannibals and pirates were seldom serious threats to an American reader of 1901; the dangers encountered on the second trip are from evils found in our world. The French scientist and the Chicago businessman try at different times to kill Rob so they can obtain his inventions. Murder for gain, Rob learns, is part of the normal life of the world that he is supposed to improve. When he returns home (to the melodramatic news that his absence has nearly killed his mother), he refuses the Demon's last three gifts because mankind does not have the wisdom to use them properly. In this final scene, the Demon seems foolish and pitiable, while Rob has deepened his understanding of himself and of the flaws of mankind.

Baum, like many modern writers of both fantasy and science fiction, had an ambivalent attitude toward scientific advance. Baum was fascinated by technology, as befitted a man strongly of the progressive era, and he is the most important fantasy writer to base his secondary world on technology. Many of his finest creations utilized machinery. Mechanical men — early robots — appear in *A New Wonderland* (written in 1896 but not published until 1900) and *Father Goose, His Book* (1899), before reaching their highest development in two of the great fairy tale characters: the Tin Woodman (first appearing in 1900 in *The Wonderful Wizard of Oz*) and Tik-Tok (who made his debut in 1907 in *Ozma of Oz*). And there are several minor mechanical characters, including Mr. Split of *Dot and Tot of Merryland*, the Giant with the Hammer of *Ozma of Oz*, and the Tin Soldier of *The Tin Woodman of Oz* (1918). Many of the marvels of Oz are glorified mechanical gadgets. Using "machinery and air-pumps," the Wizard blows gigantic bubbles made of soap and glue by which he sends home Ozma's birthday guests in *The Road to Oz* (1909). In his posthumous *Glinda of Oz* (1920), the island of the Skeezers is raised and lowered by a huge machine of wheels and gears which is operated by magic powder and incantations. In the same book, Glinda uses for magical purposes an apparently scientific instrument called a skeropythrope.[2]

Baum was usually optimistic about scientific progress; he indicates in the preface to *The Lost Princess of Oz* his belief that technology will lead to "the betterment of the world." But there is in some of his books a dislike of the changes brought about by civilization, which Baum seems to equate with the industrial revolution. Various fantasy lands are fortunate because they have not been civilized. The clearest example of this attitude is in the opening chapter of *The Enchanted Island of Yew* (1903): "In the old days, when the world was young, there were no automobiles nor flying-machines to make one wonder; nor were there railway trains, nor telephones, nor mechanical inventions of any sort to keep people keyed up to a high pitch of excitement. Men and women lived simply and quietly. They were Nature's children, and breathed fresh air into their lungs instead of smoke and coal gas; and tramped through green meadows and deep forests instead of riding in street cars; and went to bed when it grew dark and rose with the sun — which is vastly different from the present custom." Baum however, was not certain in *Yew* that progress was completely bad. At the conclusion of the book he says with entire seriousness that "civilization had won the people, and they no longer robbed or fought or indulged in magical arts, but were busily employed and leading respectable lives."

Baum treated scientific advance with sardonic humor in *John Dough and the Cherub* (1906). John Dough, a gingerbread man, meets Chick the Cherub, an "incubator baby," on the Island of Phreex, which bears some resemblance to the Academy of Lagado in the third book of *Gulliver's Travels*. In Phreex John Dough becomes acquainted with an inventor who decides that umbrellas hardly do the job they were made for, and thus has invented a new method to keep dry in the rain. It is a little

---

Electricity appears in *Tik-Tok of Oz* (1914) in Electra, one of the six maidens who serve the Queen of Light. Here electricity seems mystical rather than technological, although Baum would probably consider such a distinction artificial.

tube which works on the same principle as Rob's flying device: "within this tube is stored a Power of Repulsion that overcomes the Attraction of Gravitation, and sends the raindrops flying upward again." Unfortunately the tube does not work for very long periods of time, a fact which does not disturb the inventor at all. Baum does not, however, condemn all scientific advance in *John Dough*; the gingerbread man meets two successful inventors in Phreex, and he and the Cherub escape the island through one of their inventions, a strange sort of flying machine.

The seeming inconsistencies in Baum's attitude toward science and technology are resolved in *The Master Key*. He is pessimistic about the results of scientific advance as long as man is incapable of using science wisely; that is the lesson which Rob learns when he realizes that some people are willing to murder him for possession of the inventions. But Baum is optimistic that someday man will be able to produce good results from science. The story ends with the Demon waiting for mankind to become "intelligent enough and advanced enough" to strike the master key again. What happens when man has reached that level is described in the Oz books; under the wise leaders like Glinda, Ozma, and the Wizard, science has benefited man. It has not produced the smoke and filth described in the first chapter of *The Enchanted Island of Yew*. But our world is closer to *The Master Key* than it is to Oz, and Baum fears that, unless human nature changes, scientific advances may produce disaster.

After two world wars, it is difficult for us to share Baum's optimism that someday man will be able to handle his discoveries wisely. Scientific advances have gone beyond almost everything Baum imagined, but there is no sign that man's flawed moral nature has changed. Technology has brought great material benefit and with it the devastation of Hiroshima and southeast Asia. We may not be able to accept Baum's optimism, qualified though it is, but his warning about the misuse of knowledge will always remain valid.

CONTENTS

CONTENTS

ILLUSTRATIONS

ILLUSTRATIONS

ILLUSTRATIONS

ILLUSTRATIONS

ILLUSTRATIONS

WHO KNOWS?

These things are quite improbable, to be sure; but are they impossible?

Our big world rolls over as smoothly as it did centuries ago, without a squeak to show it needs oiling after all these years of revolution. But times change because men change, and because civilization, like John Brown's soul, goes ever marching on.

The impossibilities of yesterday become the accepted facts of to-day.

Here is a fairy tale founded upon the wonders of electricity and written for children of this generation. Yet when my readers shall have become men and women my story may not seem to their children like a fairy tale at all.

Perhaps one, perhaps two—perhaps several of the Demon's devices will be, by that time, in popular use.

Who knows?

"*In wonder all philosophy began; in wonder it all ends; and admiration fills up the interspace. But the first wonder is the offspring of ignorance: the last is the parent of adoration.*'

—COLERIDGE.

THE MASTER KEY

CHAPTER ONE

ROB'S WORKSHOP

WHEN Rob became interested in electricity his clear-headed father considered the boy's fancy to be instructive as well as amusing; so he heartily encouraged his son, and Rob never lacked batteries, motors or supplies of any sort that his experiments might require.

He fitted up the little back room in the attic as his workshop, and from thence a net-work of wires soon ran throughout the house. Not only had every outside door its

1

electric bell, but every window was fitted
with a burglar alarm; moreover no one could
cross the threshold of any interior room without registering the fact in Rob's workshop.
The gas was lighted by an electric fob; a
chime, connected with an erratic clock in the
boy's room, woke the servants at all hours
of the night and caused the cook to give
warning; a bell rang whenever the postman
dropped a letter into the box; there were
bells, bells, bells everywhere, ringing at the
right time, the wrong time and all the time.
And there were telephones in the different
rooms, too, through which Rob could call
up the different members of the family just
when they did not wish to be disturbed.

His mother and sisters soon came to vote
the boy's scientific craze a nuisance; but
his father was delighted with these evi-
dences of Rob's skill as an electrician, and
insisted that he be allowed perfect freedom
in carrying out his ideas.

"Electricity," said the old gentleman,

sagely, "is destined to become the motive power of the world. The future advance of civilization will be along electrical lines. Our boy may become a great inventor and astonish the world with his wonderful creations."

"And in the meantime," said the mother, despairingly, "we shall all be electrocuted, or the house burned down by crossed wires, or we shall be blown into eternity by an explosion of chemicals!"

"Nonsense!" ejaculated the proud father. "Rob's storage batteries are not powerful enough to electrocute one or set the house on fire. Do give the boy a chance, Belinda."

"And his pranks are so humiliating," continued the lady. "When the minister called yesterday and rang the bell a big card appeared on the front door on which was printed the words: 'Busy; Call Again.' Fortunately Helen saw him and let him in, but when I reproved Robert for the act he

3

said he was just trying the sign to see if it
would work."

"Exactly! The boy is an inventor already. I shall have one of those cards attached to the door of my private office at
once. I tell you, Belinda, our son will be
a great man one of these days," said Mr.
Joslyn, walking up and down with pom-
pous strides and almost bursting with the
pride he took in his young hopeful.

Mrs. Joslyn sighed. She knew remon-
strance was useless so long as her husband
encouraged the boy, and that she would be
wise to bear her cross with fortitude.

Rob also knew his mother's protests
would be of no avail; so he continued to
revel in electrical processes of all sorts, using
the house as an experimental station to test
the powers of his productions.

It was in his own room, however,—his
"workshop"—that he especially delighted.
For not only was it the center of all his
numerous "lines" throughout the house,

4

but he had rigged up therein a wonderful
array of devices for his own amusement.
A trolley-car moved around a circular track
and stopped regularly at all stations; an en-
gine and train of cars moved jerkily up and
down a steep grade and through a tunnel;
a windmill was busily pumping water from
the dishpan into the copper skillet; a saw-
mill was in full operation and a host of mechanical blacksmiths, scissors-grinders, car-
penters, wood-choppers and millers were
connected with a motor which kept them
working away at their trades in awkward
but persevering fashion.

The room was crossed and recrossed with
wires. They crept up the walls, lined the
floor, made a grille of the ceiling and would
catch an unwary visitor under the chin or
above the ankle just when he least expected
it. Yet visitors were forbidden in so crowded
a room, and even his father declined to go
farther than the doorway. As for Rob, he
thought he knew all about the wires, and

what each one was for; but they puzzled
even him, at times, and he was often perplexed to know how to utilize them all.

One day when he had locked himself in
to avoid interruption while he planned the
electrical illumination of a gorgeous paste-
board palace, he really became confused
over the network of wires. He had a "switch-
board," to be sure, where he could make
and break connections as he chose; but the
wires had somehow become mixed, and he
could not tell what combinations to use to
throw the power on to his miniature electric
lights.

So he experimented in a rather haphaz-
ard fashion, connecting this and that wire
blindly and by guesswork, in the hope that
he would strike the right combination.
Then he thought the combination might be
right and there was a lack of power; so he
added other lines of wire to his connections,
and still others, until he had employed
almost every wire in the room.

6

A quick flash of light almost blinded Rob

Yet it would not work; and after pausing a moment to try to think what was wrong he went at it again, putting this and that line into connection, adding another here and another there, until suddenly, as he made a last change, a quick flash of light almost blinded him, and the switch-board crackled ominously, as if struggling to carry a powerful current.

Rob covered his face at the flash, but finding himself unhurt he took away his hands and with blinking eyes attempted to look at a wonderful radiance which seemed to fill the room, making it many times brighter than the brightest day.

Although at first completely dazzled, he peered before him until he discovered that the light was concentrated near one spot, from which all the glorious rays seemed to scintillate.

He closed his eyes a moment to rest them; then re-opening them and shading them somewhat with his hands, he made out the

7

form of a curious Being standing with majesty and composure in the center of the
magnificent radiance and looking down
upon him!

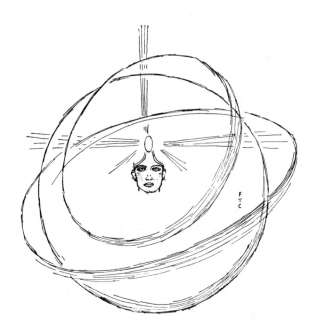

CHAPTER TWO

THE DEMON OF ELECTRICITY

ROB was a courageous boy, but a thrill of fear passed over him in spite of his bravest endeavor as he gazed upon the wondrous apparition that confronted him. For several moments he sat as if turned to stone, so motionless was he; but his eyes were nevertheless fastened upon the Being and devouring every detail of his appearance.

And how strange an appearance he presented!

His jacket was a wavering mass of white light, edged with braid of red flames that

shot little tongues in all directions. The
buttons blazed in golden fire. His trousers
had a bluish, incandescent color, with
glowing stripes of crimson braid. His vest
was gorgeous with all the colors of the rain-
bow blended into a flashing, resplendent
mass. In feature he was most majestic, and
his eyes held the soft but penetrating bril-
liance of electric lights.

It was hard to meet the gaze of those
searching eyes, but Rob did it, and at once
the splendid apparition bowed and said in
a low, clear voice:

"I am here."

"I know that," answered the boy, trembling, "but *why* are you here?"

"Because you have touched the Master
Key of Electricity, and I must obey the
laws of nature that compel me to respond
to your summons."

"I—I didn't know I touched the Master
Key," faltered the boy.

"I understand that. You did it unconsciously. No one in the world has ever done it before, for Nature has hitherto kept the secret safe locked within her bosom."

Rob took time to wonder at this statement.

" Then who are you?" he inquired, at length.

" The Demon of Electricity," was the solemn answer.

" Good gracious !" exclaimed Rob, " a demon !"

" Certainly. I am, in truth, the Slave of the Master Key, and am forced to obey the commands of any one who is wise and brave enough—or, as in your own case, fortunate and fool-hardy enough—to touch it."

" I—I've never guessed there was such a thing as a Master Key, or—or a Demon of Electricity, and—and I'm awfully sorry I—I called you up !" stammered the boy, abashed by the imposing appearance of his companion.

11

The Demon actually smiled at this speech,
—a smile that was almost reassuring.

"I am not sorry," he said, in kindlier
tone, "for it is not much pleasure waiting
century after century for some one to command my services. I have often thought
my existence uncalled for, since you Earth
people are so stupid and ignorant that you
seem unlikely ever to master the secret of
electrical power."

"Oh, we have some great masters among
us!" cried Rob, rather nettled at this statement. "Now, there's Edison—"

"Edison!" exclaimed the Demon, with a
faint sneer; "what does he know?"

"Lots of things," declared the boy.
"He's invented no end of wonderful
electrical things."

"You are wrong to call them wonderful," replied the Demon, lightly. "He
really knows little more than yourself about
the laws that control electricity. His inventions are trifling things in comparison with

the really wonderful results to be obtained by one who would actually know how to direct the electric powers instead of groping blindly after insignificant effects. Why, I've stood for months by Edison's elbow, hoping and longing for him to touch the Master Key; but I can see plainly he will never accomplish it."

"Then there's Tesla," said the boy.

The Demon laughed.

"There is Tesla, to be sure," he said. "But what of him?"

"Why, he's discovered a powerful light," the Demon gave an amused chuckle, " and he's in communication with the people in Mars."

"What people?"

"Why, the people who live there."

"There are none."

This quiet statement almost took Rob's breath away, and caused him to stare hard at his visitor.

"It's generally thought," he resumed, in

13

an annoyed tone, "that Mars has inhabitants who are far in advance of ourselves in civilization. Many scientific men think the people of Mars have been trying to signal us for years, only we don't understand their signals. And great novelists have written about the Martians and their wonderful civilization, and—"

"And they all know as much about that little planet as you do yourself," interrupted the Demon, impatiently. "The trouble with you Earth people is that you delight in guessing about what you can not know. Now I happen to know all about Mars, because I can traverse all space and have had ample leisure to investigate the different planets. Mars is not peopled at all, nor is any other of the planets you recognize in the heavens. Some contain low orders of beasts, to be sure, but Earth alone has an intelligent, thinking, reasoning population, and your scientists and novelists would do better trying to comprehend their own planet than in groping through space to unravel the mysteries of barren and unimportant worlds."

Rob listened to this with surprise and disappointment; but he reflected that the Demon ought to know what he was talking about, so he did not venture to contradict him.

"It is really astonishing," continued the Apparition, "how little you people have learned about electricity. It is an Earth element that has existed since the Earth itself was formed, and if you but understood its proper use humanity would be marvelously benefited in many ways."

"We are, already," protested Rob; "our discoveries in electricity have enabled us to live much more conveniently."

"Then imagine your condition were you able fully to control this great element," replied the other, gravely. "The weaknesses and privations of mankind would be converted into power and luxury."

" That's true, Mr.—Mr.—Demon," said the boy. " Excuse me if I don't get your name right, but I understood you to say you are a demon."

" Certainly. The Demon of Electricity."

" But electricity is a good thing, you know, and—and—"

" Well ?"

" I've always understood that demons were bad things," added Rob, boldly.

" Not necessarily," returned his visitor. " If you will take the trouble to consult your dictionary, you will find that demons may be either good or bad, like any other class of beings. Originally all demons were good, yet of late years people have come to consider all demons evil. I do not know why. Should you read Hesiod you will find he says:

' Soon was a world of holy demons made,
Aerial spirits, by great Jove designed
To be on earth the guardians of mankind.' "

16

" But Jove was himself a myth," objected Rob, who had been studying mythology.

The Demon shrugged his shoulders.

" Then take the words of Mr. Shakespeare, to whom you all defer," he replied. "Do you not remember that he says:

> ' Thy demon (that's thy spirit which keeps thee) is
> Noble, courageous, high, unmatchable.' "

" Oh, if Shakespeare says it, that's all right," answered the boy. " But it seems you're more like a genius, for you answer the summons of the Master Key of Electricity in the same way Aladdin's genius answered the rubbing of the lamp."

" To be sure. A demon is also a genius; and a genius is a demon," said the Being. " What matters a name? I am here to do your bidding."

CHAPTER THREE

THE THREE GIFTS

FAMILIARITY with any great thing removes our awe of it. The great general is only terrible to the enemy; the great poet is frequently scolded by his wife; the children of the great statesman clamber about his knees with perfect trust and impunity; the great actor who is called before the curtain by admiring audiences is often waylaid at the stage door by his creditors.

So Rob, having conversed for a time with the glorious Demon of Electricity, began to regard him with more composure and less awe, as his eyes grew more and more ac-

customed to the splendor that at first had
well-nigh blinded them.

When the Demon announced himself
ready to do the boy's bidding, he frankly
replied:

"I am no skilled electrician, as you
very well know. My calling you here was
an accident. So I don't know how to command you, nor what to ask you to do."

"But I must not take advantage of your
ignorance," answered the Demon. "Also,
I am quite anxious to utilize this opportunity to show the world what a powerful element electricity really is. So permit me
to inform you that, having struck the Master Key, you are at liberty to demand from
me three gifts each week for three succes-
sive weeks. These gifts, provided they are
within the scope of electricity, I will grant."

Rob shook his head regretfully.

"If I were a great electrician I should
know what to ask," he said. "But I am too

ignorant to take advantage of your kind offer."

"Then," replied the Demon, "I will myself suggest the gifts, and they will be of such a character that the Earth people will learn the possibilities that lie before them and be encouraged to work more intelligently and to persevere in mastering those natural and simple laws which control electricity. For one of the greatest errors they now labor under is that electricity is complicated and hard to understand. It is really the simplest Earth element, lying within easy reach of any one who stretches out his hand to grasp and control its powers."

Rob yawned, for he thought the Demon's speeches were growing rather tiresome. Perhaps the genius noticed this rudeness, for he continued:

"I regret, of course, that you are a boy instead of a grown man, for it will appear singular to your friends that so thoughtless a youth should seemingly have mastered the secrets that have baffled your most learned scientists. But that can not be helped, and presently you will become, through my aid, the most powerful and wonderful personage in all the world.''

"Thank you," said Rob, meekly. "It'll be no end of fun."

"Fun!" echoed the Demon, scornfully. "But never mind; I must use the material Fate has provided for me, and make the best of it."

"What will you give me first?" asked the boy, eagerly.

"That requires some thought," returned the Demon, and paused for several moments, while Rob feasted his eyes upon the gorgeous rays of color that flashed and vibrated in every direction and surrounded the figure of his visitor with an intense glow that resembled a halo.

Then the Demon raised his head and said:

"The thing most necessary to man is food to nourish his body. He passes a considerable part of his life in the struggle to procure food, to prepare it properly, and in the act of eating. This is not right. Your body can not be very valuable to you if all your time is required to feed it. I shall, therefore, present you, as my first gift, this box of tablets. Within each tablet are stored certain elements of electricity which are capable of nourishing a human body for a full day. All you need do is to toss one into your mouth each day and swallow it. It will nourish you, satisfy your hunger and build up your health and strength. The ordinary food of mankind is more or less injurious; this is entirely beneficial. Moreover, you may carry enough tablets in your pocket to last for months."

Here he presented Rob the silver box of tablets, and the boy, somewhat nervously, thanked him for the gift.

"The next requirement of man," contin-

ued the Demon, "is defense from his enemies. I notice with sorrow that men frequently have wars and kill one another.
Also, even in civilized communities, man
is in constant danger from highwaymen,
cranks and policemen. To defend himself he uses heavy and dangerous guns,
with which to destroy his enemies. This
is wrong. He has no right to take away
what he can not bestow; to destroy what
he can not create. To kill a fellow-creat-
ure is a horrid crime, even if done in self-
defense. Therefore, my second gift to you
is this little tube. You may carry it within
your pocket. Whenever an enemy threat-
ens you, be it man or beast, simply point
the tube and press this button in the handle.
An electric current will instantly be directed
upon your foe, rendering him wholly unconscious for the period of one hour. During that time you will have opportunity to
escape. As for your enemy, after regain-
ing consciousness he will suffer no incon-

23

venience from the encounter beyond a slight headache.''

"That's fine!" said Rob, as he took the tube. It was scarcely six inches long, and hollow at one end.

"The busy lives of men," proceeded the Demon, "require them to move about and travel in all directions. Yet to assist them there are only such crude and awkward machines as electric trolleys, cable cars, steam railways and automobiles. These crawl slowly over the uneven surface of the earth and frequently get out of order. It has grieved me that men have not yet discovered what even the birds know: that the atmosphere offers them swift and easy means of traveling from one part of the earth's surface to another.''

"Some people have tried to build airships," remarked Rob.

"So they have; great, unwieldy machines which offer so much resistance to the air that they are quite useless. A big machine is not needed to carry one through the air. There are forces in nature which may be readily used for such purpose. Tell me, what holds you to the Earth, and makes a stone fall to the ground?''

"Attraction of gravitation," said Rob, promptly.

"Exactly. That is one force I refer to," said the Demon. "The force of repulsion, which is little known, but just as powerful, is another that mankind may direct. Then there are the Polar electric forces, attracting objects toward the north or south poles. You have guessed something of this by the use of the compass, or electric needle. Opposed to these is centrifugal electric force, drawing objects from east to west, or in the opposite direction. This force is created by the whirl of the earth upon its axis, and is easily utilized, although your scientific men have as yet paid little attention to it.

"These forces, operating in all directions, absolute and immutable, are at the disposal

of mankind. They will carry you through
the atmosphere wherever and whenever you
choose. That is, if you know how to control them. Now, here is a machine I have
myself perfected.''

The Demon drew from his pocket something that resembled an open-faced watch,
having a narrow, flexible band attached to it.

''When you wish to travel,'' said he,
''attach this little machine to your left wrist
by means of the band. It is very light and
will not be in your way. On this dial are
points marked 'up' and 'down' as well
as a perfect compass. When you desire to
rise into the air set the indicator to the word
'up,' using a finger of your right hand to
turn it. When you have risen as high as
you wish, set the indicator to the point of
the compass you want to follow and you
will be carried by the proper electric force
in that direction. To descend, set the indicator to the word 'down.' Do you understand?''

"Perfectly!" cried Rob, taking the machine from the Demon with unfeigned delight. "This is really wonderful, and I'm awfully obliged to you!"

"Don't mention it," returned the Demon, dryly. "These three gifts you may amuse yourself with for the next week. It seems hard to entrust such great scientific discoveries to the discretion of a mere boy; but they are quite harmless, so if you exercise proper care you can not get into trouble through their possession. And who knows what benefits to humanity may result? One week from to-day, at this hour, I will again appear to you, at which time you shall receive the second series of electrical gifts."

"I'm not sure," said Rob, "that I shall be able again to make the connections that will strike the Master Key."

"Probably not," answered the Demon. "Could you accomplish that, you might command my services forever. But, having once succeeded, you are entitled to the

nine gifts—three each week for three weeks
—so you have no need to call me to do my
duty. I shall appear of my own accord."

"Thank you," murmured the boy.

The Demon bowed and spread his hands
in the form of a semi-circle. An instant
later there was a blinding flash, and when
Rob recovered from it and opened his eyes
the Demon of Electricity had disappeared.

CHAPTER FOUR

TESTING THE INSTRUMENTS

THERE is little doubt that had this strange experience befallen a grown man he would have been stricken with a fit of trembling or a sense of apprehension, or even fear, at the thought of having faced the terrible Demon of Electricity, of having struck the Master Key of the world's greatest natural forces, and finding himself possessed of three such wonderful and useful gifts. But a boy takes everything as a matter of course. As the tree of knowledge sprouts and expands within him, shooting out leaf after leaf of practical experience, the succession of surprises dulls his faculty of wonderment. It takes a great deal to startle a boy.

Rob was full of delight at his unexpected good fortune; but he did not stop to consider that there was anything remarkably queer or uncanny in the manner in which it had come to him. His chief sensation was one of pride. He would now be able to surprise those who had made fun of his electrical craze and force them to respect his marvelous powers. He decided to say nothing about the Demon or the accidental striking of the Master Key. In exhibiting to his friends the electrical devices he had acquired it would be "no end of fun" to mark their amazement and leave them to guess how he performed his feats.

So he put his treasures into his pocket, locked his workshop and went downstairs to his room to prepare for dinner.

While brushing his hair he remembered it was no longer necessary for him to eat ordinary food. He was feeling quite hungry at that moment, for he had a boy's ravenous appetite; but, taking the silver box from his pocket, he swallowed a tablet and at once felt his hunger as fully satisfied as if he had partaken of a hearty meal, while at the same time he experienced an exhilarating glow throughout his body and a clearness of brain and gaiety of spirits which filled him with intense gratification.

Still, he entered the dining-room when the bell rang and found his father and mother and sisters already assembled there.

"Where have you been all day, Robert?" inquired his mother.

"No need to ask," said Mr. Joslyn, with a laugh. "Fussing over electricity, I'll bet a cookie!"

"I do wish," said the mother, fretfully, "that he would get over that mania. It unfits him for anything else."

"Precisely," returned her husband, dishing the soup; "but it fits him for a great

career when he becomes a man. Why
shouldn't he spend his summer vacation in
pursuit of useful knowledge instead of romp-
ing around like ordinary boys?"

" No soup, thank you," said Rob.

" What !" exclaimed his father, looking
at him in surprise, " it's your favorite
soup."

" I know," said Rob, quietly, " but I
don't want any."

"Are you ill, Robert?" asked his mother.

" Never felt better in my life," answered
Rob, truthfully.

Yet Mrs. Joslyn looked worried, and
when Rob refused the roast, she was really
shocked.

" Let me feel your pulse, my poor boy!"
she commanded, and wondered to find it so
regular.

In fact, Rob's action surprised them all.
He sat calmly throughout the meal, eating nothing, but apparently in good health

and spirits, while even his sisters regarded
him with troubled countenances.

"He's worked too hard, I guess," said
Mr. Joslyn, shaking his head sadly.

"Oh, no; I haven't," protested Rob;
"but I've decided not to eat anything,
hereafter. It's a bad habit, and does more
harm than good."

"Wait till breakfast," said sister Helen,
with a laugh; "you'll be hungry enough
by that time."

However, the boy had no desire for food
at breakfast time, either, as the tablet suf-
ficed for an entire day. So he renewed
the anxiety of the family by refusing to join
them at the table.

"If this goes on," Mr. Joslyn said to
his son, when breakfast was finished, "I
shall be obliged to send you away for your
health."

"I think of making a trip this morning,"
said Rob, carelessly.

"Where to?"

33

"Oh, I may go to Boston, or take a run over to Cuba or Jamaica," replied the boy.

"But you can not go so far by yourself," declared his father; "and there is no one to go with you, just now. Nor can I spare the money at present for so expensive a trip."

"Oh, it won't cost anything," replied Rob, with a smile.

Mr. Joslyn looked upon him gravely and sighed. Mrs. Joslyn bent over her son with tears in her eyes and said:

"This electrical nonsense has affected your mind, dear. You must promise me to keep away from that horrid workshop for a time."

"I won't enter it for a week," he answered. "But you needn't worry about me. I haven't been experimenting with electricity all this time for nothing, I can tell you. As for my health, I'm as well and strong as any boy need be, and there's nothing wrong with my head, either. Common folks always think great men are crazy, but Edison and Tesla and I don't pay any attention to that. We've got our discoveries to look after. Now, as I said, I'm going for a little trip in the interests of science. I may be back to-night, or I may be gone several days. Anyhow, I'll be back in a week, and you mustn't worry about me a single minute."

"How are you going?" inquired his father, in the gentle, soothing tone persons use in addressing maniacs.

"Through the air," said Rob.

His father groaned.

"Where's your balloon?" inquired sister Mabel, sarcastically.

"I don't need a balloon," returned the boy. "That's a clumsy way of traveling, at best. I shall go by electric propulsion."

"Good gracious!" cried Mr. Joslyn, and the mother murmured: "My poor boy! my poor boy!"

"As you are my nearest relatives," continued Rob, not noticing these exclamations, " I will allow you to come into the back yard and see me start. You will then understand something of my electrical powers."

They followed him at once, although with unbelieving faces, and on the way Rob clasped the little machine to his left wrist, so that his coat sleeve nearly hid it.

When they reached the lawn at the back of the house Rob kissed them all good-by, much to his sisters' amusement, and turned the indicator of the little instrument to the word " up."

Immediately he began to rise into the air.

" Don't worry about me !" he called down to them. " Good-by!"

Mrs. Joslyn, with a scream of terror, hid her face in her hands.

" He'll break his neck !" cried the astounded father, tipping back his head to look after his departing son.

"He'll break his neck!" cried the astounded father

"Come back! Come back!" shouted the girls to the soaring adventurer.

"I will—some day!" was the far-away answer.

Having risen high enough to pass over the tallest tree or steeple, Rob put the indicator to the east of the compass-dial and at once began moving rapidly in that direction.

The sensation was delightful. He rode as gently as a feather floats, without any exertion at all on his own part; yet he moved so swiftly that he easily distanced a railway train that was speeding in the same direction.

"This is great!" reflected the youth. "Here I am, traveling in fine style, without a penny to pay any one! And I've enough food to last me a month in my coat pocket. This electricity is the proper stuff, after all! And the Demon's a trump, and no mistake. Whee-ee! How small everything looks down below there. The people are bugs, and the houses are soap-boxes,

and the trees are like clumps of grass. I
seem to be passing over a town. Guess
I'll drop down a bit, and take in the sights."

He pointed the indicator to the word
"down," and at once began dropping
through the air. He experienced the sensation one feels while descending in an elevator. When he reached a point just above
the town he put the indicator to the zero
mark and remained stationary, while he
examined the place. But there was nothing
to interest him, particularly; so after a brief
survey he once more ascended and continued his journey toward the east.

At about two o'clock in the afternoon he
reached the city of Boston, and alighting
unobserved in a quiet street he walked
around for several hours enjoying the sights
and wondering what people would think of
him if they but knew his remarkable powers. But as he looked just like any other
boy no one noticed him in any way.

It was nearly evening, and Rob had wandered down by the wharves to look at the shipping, when his attention was called to an ugly looking bull dog, which ran toward him and began barking ferociously.

"Get out!" said the boy, carelessly, and made a kick at the brute.

The dog uttered a fierce growl and sprang upon him with bared teeth and flashing red eyes. Instantly Rob drew the electric tube from his pocket, pointed it at the dog and pressed the button. Almost at the same moment the dog gave a yelp, rolled over once or twice and lay still.

"I guess that'll settle him," laughed the boy; but just then he heard an angry shout, and looking around saw a policeman running toward him.

"Kill me dog, will ye—eh?" yelled the officer; "well, I'll just run ye in for that same, an' ye'll spend the night in the lock-up!" And on he came, with drawn club in one hand and a big revolver in the other.

"You'll have to catch me first," said

Rob, still laughing, and to the amazement of the policeman he began rising straight into the air.

"Come down here! Come down, or I'll shoot!" shouted the fellow, flourishing his revolver.

Rob was afraid he would; so, to avoid accidents, he pointed the tube at him and pressed the button. The red-whiskered policeman keeled over quite gracefully and fell across the body of the dog, while Rob continued to mount upward until he was out of sight of those in the streets.

"That was a narrow escape," he thought, breathing more freely. "I hated to paralyze that policeman, but he might have sent a bullet after me. Anyhow, he'll be all right again in an hour, so I needn't worry."

It was beginning to grow dark, and he wondered what he should do next. Had he possessed any money he would have descended to the town and taken a bed at a hotel, but he had left home without a single penny. Fortunately the nights were warm at this season, so he determined to travel all night, that he might reach by morning some place he had never before visited.

Cuba had always interested him, and he judged it ought to lie in a southeasterly direction from Boston. So he set the indicator to that point and began gliding swiftly toward the southeast.

He now remembered that it was twenty-four hours since he had eaten the first electrical tablet. As he rode through the air he consumed another. All hunger at once left him, while he felt the same invigorating sensations as before.

After a time the moon came out, and Rob amused himself gazing at the countless stars in the sky and wondering if the Demon was right when he said the world was the most important of all the planets.

But presently he grew sleepy, and before he realized what was happening he had fallen into a sound and peaceful slumber,

while the indicator still pointed to the southeast and he continued to move rapidly
through the cool night air.

CHAPTER FIVE

THE CANNIBAL ISLAND

DOUBTLESS the adventures of the day had tired Rob, for he slept throughout the night as comfortably as if he had been within his own room, lying upon his own bed. When, at last, he opened his eyes and gazed sleepily about him, he found himself over a great body of water, moving along with considerable speed.

"It's the ocean, of course," he said to himself. "I haven't reached Cuba yet."

I is to be regretted that Rob's knowledge of geography was so superficial; for, as he had intended to reach Cuba, he should have taken a course almost southwest from Boston, instead of southeast. The sad result of his ignorance you will presently learn, for during the entire day he continued to travel over a boundless waste of ocean, without the sight of even an island to cheer him.

The sun shone so hot that he regretted he had not brought an umbrella. But he wore a wide-brimmed straw hat, which protected him somewhat, and he finally discovered that by rising to a considerable distance above the ocean he avoided the reflection of the sun upon the water and also came within the current of good breeze.

Of course he dared not stop, for there was no place to land; so he calmly continued his journey.

"It may be I've missed Cuba," he thought; "but I can not change my course now, for if I did I might get lost, and never be able to find land again. If I keep on as I am I shall be sure to reach land of some sort, in time, and when I wish to return home I can set the indicator to the north-west and that will take me directly back to Boston."

This was good reasoning, but the rash youth had no idea he was speeding over the ocean, or that he was destined to arrive shortly at the barbarous island of Brava, off the coast of Africa. Yet such was the case; just as the sun sank over the edge of the waves he saw, to his great relief, a large island directly in his path.

He dropped to a lower position in the air, and when he judged himself to be over the center of the island he turned the indi-cator to zero and stopped short.

The country was beautifully wooded, while pretty brooks sparkled through the rich green foliage of the trees. The island sloped upwards from the sea-coast in all di-rections, rising to a hill that was almost a mountain in the center. There were two open spaces, one on each side of the island,

and Rob saw that these spaces were occupied by queer-looking huts built from brushwood and branches of trees. This showed that the island was inhabited, but as Rob had no idea what island it was he wisely determined not to meet the natives until he had discovered what they were like and whether they were disposed to be friendly.

So he moved over the hill, the top of which proved to be a flat, grass-covered plateau about fifty feet in diameter. Finding it could not be easily reached from below, on account of its steep sides, and contained neither men nor animals, he alighted on the hill-top and touched his feet to the earth for the first time in twenty-four hours.

The ride through the air had not tired him in the least; in fact, he felt as fresh and vigorous as if he had been resting throughout the journey. As he walked upon the soft grass of the plateau he felt elated, and compared himself to the explorers of ancient days; for it was evident that civilization had not yet reached this delightful spot.

There was scarcely any twilight in this tropical climate and it grew dark quickly. Within a few minutes the entire island, save where he stood, became dim and indistinct. He ate his daily tablet, and after watching the red glow fade in the western sky and the gray shadows of night settle around him he stretched himself comfortably upon the grass and went to sleep.

The events of the day must have deepened his slumber, for when he awoke the sun was shining almost directly over him, showing that the day was well advanced. He stood up, rubbed the sleep from his eyes and decided he would like a drink of water. From where he stood he could see several little brooks following winding paths through the forest, so he settled upon one that seemed farthest from the brushwood villages, and turning his indicator in that direc-

THE MASTER KEY

tion soon floated through the air to a sheltered spot upon the bank.

Kneeling down, he enjoyed a long, refreshing drink of the clear water, but as he started to regain his feet a coil of rope was suddenly thrown about him, pinning his arms to his sides and rendering him absolutely helpless.

At the same time his ears were saluted with a wild chattering in an unknown tongue, and he found himself surrounded by a group of natives of hideous appearance. They were nearly naked, and bore spears and heavy clubs as their only weapons. Their hair was long, curly, and thick as bushes, and through their noses and ears were stuck the teeth of sharks and curious metal ornaments.

These creatures had stolen upon Rob so quietly that he had not heard a sound, but now they jabbered loudly, as if much excited.

Finally one fat and somewhat aged native, who seemed to be a chief, came close to Rob and said, in broken English:

"How get here?"

"I flew," said the boy, with a grin.

The chief shook his head, saying:

"No boat come. How white man come?"

"Through the air," replied Rob, who was rather flattered at being called a "man."

The chief looked into the air with a puzzled expression and shook his head again.

"White man lie," he said calmly.

Then he held further conversation with his fellows, after which he turned to Rob and announced:

"Me see white man many times. Come in big boats. White men all bad. Make kill with bang-sticks. We kill white man with club. Then we eat white man. Dead white man good. Live white man bad!'

This did not please Rob at all. The idea of being eaten by savages had never occurred to him as a sequel to his adventures. So he said rather anxiously to the chief:

"Look here, old fellow; do you want to die?"

"Me no die. You die," was the reply.

"You'll die, too, if you eat me," said Rob. "I'm full of poison."

"Poison? Don't know poison," returned the chief, much perplexed to understand him.

"Well, poison will make you sick—awful sick. Then you'll die. I'm full of it; eat it every day for breakfast. It don't hurt white men, you see, but it kills black men quicker than the bang-stick."

The chief listened to this statement carefully, but only understood it in part. After a moment's reflection he declared:

" White man lie. Lie all time. Me eat plenty white man. Never get sick; never die." Then he added, with renewed cheerfulness: " Me eat you, too !"

Before Rob could think of a further protest, his captors caught up the end of the rope and led him away through the forest. He was tightly bound, and one strand of rope ran across the machine on his wrist and pressed it into his flesh until the pain was severe. But he resolved to be brave, whatever happened, so he stumbled along after the savages without a word.

After a brief journey they came to a village, where Rob was thrust into a brush-wood hut and thrown upon the ground, still tightly bound.

"We light fire," said the chief. "Then kill little white man. Then eat him."

With this comforting promise he went away and left Rob alone to think the matter over.

"This is tough," reflected the boy, with a groan. "I never expected to feed canni-bals. Wish I was at home with mother and dad and the girls. Wish I'd never seen the Demon of Electricity and his won-derful inventions. I was happy enough before I struck that awful Master Key. And now I'll be eaten—with salt and pepper, probably. Wonder if there'll be any gravy. Perhaps they'll boil me, with biscuits, as mother does chickens. Oh-h-h-h-h! It's just awful!"

In the midst of these depressing thoughts he became aware that something was hurting his back. After rolling over he found that he had been lying upon a sharp stone that stuck out of the earth. This gave him an idea. He rolled upon the stone again and began rubbing the rope that bound him against the sharp edge.

Outside he could hear the crackling of fagots and the roar of a newly-kindled fire, so he knew he had no time to spare. He wriggled and pushed his body right and left, right and left, sawing away at the rope, until the strain and exertion started the perspiration from every pore.

At length the rope parted, and hastily uncoiling it from his body Rob stood up and rubbed his benumbed muscles and tried to regain his lost breath. He had not freed himself a moment too soon, he found, for hearing a grunt of surprise behind him he turned around and saw a native standing in the door of the hut.

Rob laughed, for he was not a bit afraid of the blacks now. As the native made a rush toward him the boy drew the electric tube from his pocket, pointed it at the foe, and pressed the button. The fellow sank to the earth without even a groan, and lay still.

Then another black entered, followed by the fat chief. When they saw Rob at liberty, and their comrade lying apparently dead, the chief cried out in surprise, using some expressive words in his own language.

"If it's just the same to you, old chap," said Rob, coolly, "I won't be eaten to-day. You can make a pie of that fellow on the ground."

"No! We eat you," cried the chief, angrily. "You cut rope, but no get away; no boat!"

"I don't need a boat, thank you," said the boy; and then, as the other native sprang forward, he pointed the tube and laid him out beside his first victim.

At this act the chief stood an instant in amazed uncertainty. Then he turned and rushed from the hut.

Laughing with amusement at the waddling, fat figure, Rob followed the chief and found himself standing almost in the center of the native village. A big fire was blazing merrily and the blacks were busy making preparations for a grand feast.

Rob was quickly surrounded by a crowd of the villagers, who chattered fiercely and made threatening motions in his direction; but as the chief cried out to them a warning in the native tongue they kept a respectful distance and contented themselves with brandishing their spears and clubs.

"If any of your fellows come nearer,"

Rob said to the fat chief, "I'll knock 'em over."

"What you make do?" asked the chief, nervously.

"Watch sharp, and you'll see," answered Rob. Then he made a mocking bow to the circle and continued: "I'm pleased to have met you fellows, and proud to think you like me well enough to want to eat me; but I'm in a bit of a hurry to-day, so I can't stop to be digested." After which, as the crowd broke into a hum of surprise, he added: "Good-day, black folks!" and quickly turned the indicator of his traveling machine to the word "up."

Slowly he rose into the air, until his heels were just above the gaping blacks; but there he stopped short. With a thrill of fear he glanced at the indicator. It was pointed properly, and he knew at once that something was wrong with the delicate mechanism that controlled it. Probably the pressure of the rope across its face, when he was bound, had put it out of order. There he was, seven feet in the air, but without the power to rise an inch farther.

This short flight, however, had greatly astonished the blacks, who, seeing his body suspended in mid-air, immediately hailed him as a god, and prostrated themselves upon the ground before him.

The fat chief had seen something of white men in his youth, and had learned to mistrust them. So, while he remained as prostrate as the rest, he peeped at Rob with one of his little black eyes and saw that the boy was ill at ease, and seemed both annoyed and frightened.

So he muttered some orders to the man next him, who wriggled along the ground until he had reached a position behind Rob, when he rose and pricked the suspended " god " with the point of his spear.

" Ouch!" yelled the boy; " stop that !"

He twisted his head around, and seeing the black again make a movement with the spear, Rob turned his electric tube upon him and keeled him over like a ten-pin.

The natives, who had looked up at his cry of pain, again prostrated themselves, kicking their toes against the ground in a terrified tattoo at this new evidence of the god's powers.

The situation was growing somewhat strained by this time, and Rob did not know what the savages would decide to do next; so he thought it best to move away from them, since he was unable to rise to a greater height. He turned the indicator towards the south, where a level space appeared between the trees; but instead of taking that direction he moved towards the northeast, a proof that his machine had now become absolutely unreliable. Moreover, he was slowly approaching the fire, which, although it had ceased blazing, was a mass of glowing red embers.

In his excitement he turned the indicator this way and that, trying to change the direction of his flight, but the only result of his endeavor was to carry him directly over the fire, where he came to a full stop.

" Murder! Help! Fire and blazes!" he cried, as he felt the glow of the coals beneath him. " I'll be roasted, after all! Here; help, Fatty, help !"

The fat chief sprang to his feet and came to the rescue. He reached up, caught Rob by the heels, and pulled him down to the ground, away from the fire. But the next moment, as he clung to the boy's feet, they both soared into the air again, and, although now far enough from the fire to escape its heat, the savage, finding himself lifted from the earth, uttered a scream of horror and let go of Rob, to fall head over heels upon the ground.

The other blacks had by this time regained their feet, and now they crowded around their chief and set him upright again.

Rob continued to float in the air, just

above their heads, and now abandoned all
thoughts of escaping by means of his
wrecked traveling machine. But he resolved to regain a foothold upon the earth
and take his chances of escape by running
rather than flying. So he turned the indicator to the word " down," and very slowly
it obeyed, allowing him, to his great relief,
to sink gently to the ground.

CHAPTER SIXTH

THE BUCCANEERS

ONCE more the blacks formed a circle around our adventurer, who coolly drew his tube and said to the chief:

"Tell your people I'm going to walk away through those trees, and if any one dares to interfere with me I'll paralyze him."

The chief understood enough English to catch his meaning, and repeated the message to his men. Having seen the terrible effect of the electric tube they wisely fell back and allowed the boy to pass.

He marched through their lines with a

fine air of dignity, although he was fearful lest some of the blacks should stick a spear into him or bump his head with a war-club. But they were awed by the wonders they had seen and were still inclined to believe him a god, so he was not molested.

When he found himself outside the village he made for the high plateau in the center of the island, where he could be safe from the cannibals while he collected his thoughts. But when he reached the place he found the sides so steep he could not climb them, so he adjusted the indicator to the word "up" and found it had still enough power to support his body while he clambered up the rocks to the level, grass-covered space at the top.

Then, reclining upon his back, he gave himself up to thoughts of how he might escape from his unpleasant predicament.

"Here I am, on a cannibal island, hundreds of miles from civilization, with no way to get back," he reflected. "The family will look for me every day, and finally decide I've broken my neck. The Demon will call upon me when the week is up and won't find me at home; so I'll miss the next three gifts. I don't mind that so much, for they might bring me into worse scrapes than this. But how am I to get away from this beastly island? I'll be eaten, after all, if I don't look out!"

These and similar thoughts occupied him for some time, yet in spite of much planning and thinking he could find no practical means of escape.

At the end of an hour he looked over the edge of the plateau and found it surrounded by a ring of the black cannibals, who had calmly seated themselves to watch his movements.

"Perhaps they intend to starve me into surrender," he thought; "but they won't succeed so long as my tablets hold out. And if, in time, they should starve me, I'll be too thin and tough to make good eating; so I'll get the best of them, anyhow."

Then he again lay down and began to examine his electrical traveling machine. He did not dare take it apart, fearing he might not be able to get it together again, for he knew nothing at all about its construction. But he discovered two little dents on the edge, one on each side, which had evidently been caused by the pressure of the rope.

"If I could get those dents out," he thought, "the machine might work."

He first tried to pry out the edges with his pocket knife, but the attempt resulted in failure. Then, as the sides seemed a little bulged outward by the dents, he placed the machine between two flat stones and pressed them together until the little instrument was nearly round again. The dents remained, to be sure, but he hoped he had removed the pressure upon the works.

There was just one way to discover how well he had succeeded, so he fastened the machine to his wrist and turned the indicator to the word "up."

Slowly he ascended, this time to a height of nearly twenty feet. Then his progress became slower and finally ceased altogether.

"That's a little better," he thought. "Now let's see if it will go sidewise."

He put the indicator to "north-west,"— the direction of home—and very slowly the machine obeyed and carried him away from the plateau and across the island.

The natives saw him go, and springing to their feet began uttering excited shouts and throwing their spears at him. But he was already so high and so far away that they failed to reach him, and the boy continued his journey unharmed.

Once the branches of a tall tree caught him and nearly tipped him over; but he managed to escape others by drawing up his feet. At last he was free of the island and traveling over the ocean again. He was not at all sorry to bid good-by to the cannibal island, but he was worried about the machine, which clearly was not in good working order. The vast ocean was beneath him, and he moved no faster than an ordinary walk.

"At this rate I'll get home some time next year," he grumbled. " However, I suppose I ought to be glad the machine works at all." And he really was glad.

All the afternoon and all the long summer night he moved slowly over the water. It was annoying to go at " a reg'lar jog-trot," as Rob called it, after his former swift flight; but there was no help for it.

Just as dawn was breaking he saw in the distance a small vessel, sailing in the direction he was following, yet scarcely moving for lack of wind. He soon caught up with it, but saw no one on deck, and the craft had a dingy and uncared-for appearance that was not reassuring. But after hovering over it for some time Rob decided to board the ship and rest for a while. He alighted near the bow, where the deck was highest, and was about to explore the place when a man came out of the low cabin and espied him.

This person had a most villainous countenance, and was dark-skinned, black-bearded and dressed in an outlandish, piratical costume. On seeing the boy he gave a loud shout and was immediately joined by four companions, each as disagreeable in appearance as the first.

Rob knew there would be trouble the moment he looked at this evil crew, and when they drew their daggers and pistols and began fiercely shouting in an unknown tongue, the boy sighed and took the electric tube from his coat pocket.

The buccaneers did not notice the movement, but rushed upon him so quickly that he had to press the button at a lively rate.

It was a strange sight to see the pirates drop to the
deck and lie motionless

The tube made no noise at all, so it was a strange and remarkable sight to see the pirates suddenly drop to the deck and lie motionless. Indeed, one was so nearly upon him when the electric current struck him that his head, in falling, bumped into Rob's stomach and sent him reeling against the side of the vessel.

He quickly recovered himself, and seeing his enemies were rendered harmless, the boy entered the cabin and examined it curiously. It was dirty and ill-smelling enough, but the corners and spare berths were heaped with merchandise of all kinds which had been taken from those so un-lucky as to have met these cruel and des-perate men.

After a short inspection of the place he returned to the deck and again seated him-self in the bow.

The crippled condition of his traveling machine was now his chief trouble, and although a good breeze had sprung up to fill the sails and the little bark was making fair headway, Rob knew he could never expect to reach home unless he could discover a better mode of conveyance than this.

He unstrapped the machine from his wrist to examine it better, and while holding it carelessly in his hand it slipped and fell with a bang to the deck, striking upon its round edge and rolling quickly past the cabin and out of sight. With a cry of alarm he ran after it, and after much search found it lying against the bulwark near the edge of a scupper hole, where the least jar of the ship would have sent it to the bottom of the ocean. Rob hastily seized his treasure, and upon examining it found the fall had bulged the rim so that the old dents scarcely showed at all. But its original shape was more distorted than ever, and Rob feared he had utterly ruined its delicate mechanism. Should this prove to be true, he might now consider himself a prisoner of this piratical band, the members of which, although temporarily disabled, would soon regain consciousness.

He sat in the bow, sadly thinking of his misfortunes, until he noticed that one of the men began to stir. The effect of the electric shock conveyed by the tube was beginning to wear away, and now the buccaneer sat up, rubbed his head in a bewildered fashion and looked around him. When he saw Rob he gave a shout of rage and drew his knife, but one motion of the electric tube made him cringe and slip away to the cabin, where he remained out of danger.

And now the other four sat up, groaning and muttering in their outlandish speech; but they had no notion of facing Rob's tube a second time, so one by one they joined their leader in the cabin, leaving the boy undisturbed.

By this time the ship had begun to pitch and toss in an uncomfortable fashion, and Rob noticed that the breeze had increased to a gale. There being no one to look after the sails, the vessel was in grave danger of capsizing or breaking her masts. The waves were now running high, too, and Rob began to be worried.

Presently the captain of the pirates stuck his head out of the cabin door, jabbered some unintelligible words and pointed to the sails. The boy nodded, for he understood they wanted to attend to the rigging. So the crew trooped forth, rather fearfully, and began to reef the sails and put the ship into condition to weather the storm.

Rob paid no further attention to them. He looked at his traveling machine rather doubtfully and wondered if he dared risk its power to carry him through the air. Whether he remained in the ship or trusted to the machine, he stood a good chance of dropping into the sea at any moment. So, while he hesitated, he attached the machine to his wrist and leaned over the bulwarks to watch the progress of the storm.

He might stay in the ship until it foundered, he thought, and then take his chances with the machine. He decided to wait until a climax arrived.

The climax came the next moment, for while he leaned over the bulwarks the buccaneers stole up behind him and suddenly seized him in their grasp. While two of them held his arms the others searched his pockets, taking from him the electric tube and the silver box containing his tablets. These they carried to the cabin and threw upon the heap of other valuables they had stolen. They did not notice his traveling machine, however, but seeing him now unarmed they began jeering and laughing at him, while the brutal captain relieved his anger by giving the prisoner several malicious kicks.

Rob bore his misfortune meekly, although he was almost ready to cry with grief and disappointment. But when one of the pi-

rates, to inflict further punishment on the
boy, came towards him with a heavy strap,
he resolved not to await the blow.

Turning the indicator to the word "up"
he found, to his joy and relief, that it would
yet obey the influence of the power of repulsion. Seeing him rise into the air the
fellow made a grab for his foot and held
it firmly, while his companions ran to help
him. Weight seemed to make no difference
in the machine; it lifted the pirate as well
as Rob; it lifted another who clung to the
first man's leg, and another who clung to
him. The other two also caught hold,
hoping their united strength would pull
him down, and the next minute Rob was
soaring through the air with the entire
string of five buccaneers dangling from his
left leg.

At first the villains were too astounded to
speak, but as they realized that they were
being carried through the air and away from
their ship they broke into loud shouts of

dismay, and finally the one who grasped Rob's leg lost his hold and the five plunged downward and splashed into the sea.

Finding the machine disposed to work accurately, Rob left the buccaneers to swim to the ship in the best way they could, while he dropped down to the deck again and recovered from the cabin his box of tablets and the electric tube. The fellows were just scrambling on board when he again escaped, shooting into the air with considerable speed.

Indeed, the instrument now worked better than at any time since he had reached the cannibal island, and the boy was greatly delighted.

The wind at first sent him spinning away to the south, but he continued to rise until he was above the air currents, and the storm raged far beneath him. Then he set the indicator to the northwest and breathlessly waited to see if it would obey. Hurrah! away he sped at a fair rate of speed, while all his anxiety changed to a feeling of sweet contentment.

His success had greatly surprised him, but he concluded that the jar caused by dropping the instrument had relieved the pressure upon the works, and so helped rather than harmed the free action of the electric currents.

While he moved through the air with an easy, gliding motion he watched with much interest the storm raging below. Above his head the sun was peacefully shining and the contrast was strange and impressive. After an hour or so the storm abated, or else he passed away from it, for the deep blue of the ocean again greeted his eyes. He dropped downward until he was about a hundred feet above the water, when he continued his northwesterly course.

But now he regretted having interfered for a moment with the action of the machine, for his progress, instead of being swift as a bird's flight, became slow and jerky, nor was he sure that the damaged machine might not break down altogether at any moment. Yet so far his progress was in the right direction, and he resolved to experiment no further with the instrument, but to let it go as it would, so long as it supported him above the water. However irregular the motion might be, it was sure, if continued, to bring him to land in time, and that was all he cared about just then.

When night fell his slumber was broken and uneasy, for he wakened more than once with a start of fear that the machine had broken and he was falling into the sea. Sometimes he was carried along at a swift pace, and again the machine scarcely worked at all; so his anxiety was excusable.

The following day was one of continued uneasiness for the boy, who began to be harrassed by doubts as to whether, after all, he was moving in the right direction. The machine had failed at one time in this respect and it might again. He had lost all confidence in its accuracy.

In spite of these perplexities Rob passed the second night of his uneven flight in profound slumber, being exhausted by the strain and excitement he had undergone. When he awoke at daybreak, he saw, to his profound delight, that he was approaching land.

The rising sun found him passing over a big city, which he knew to be Boston.

He did not stop. The machine was so little to be depended upon that he dared make no halt. But he was obliged to alter the direction from northwest to west, and the result of this slight change was so great a reduction in speed that it was mid-day before he saw beneath him the familiar village in which he lived.

Carefully marking the location of his father's house, he, came to a stop directly over it, and a few moments later he man-

aged to land upon the **exact** spot in the back
yard whence he had taken his first successful flight.

CHAPTER SEVEN

THE DEMON BECOMES ANGRY

WHEN Rob had been hugged and kissed by his mother and sisters, and even Mr. Joslyn had embraced him warmly, he gave them a brief account of his adventures. The story was received with many doubtful looks and much grave shaking of heads, as was quite natural under the circumstances.

" I hope, my dear son," said his father, " that you have now passed through enough dangers to last you a lifetime, so that hereafter you will be contented to remain at home."

"Oh, Robert!" cried his mother, with tears in her loving eyes, "you don't know how we've all worried about you for the past week!"

"A week?" asked Rob, with surprise.

"Yes; it's a week to-morrow morning since you flew into the air and disappeared."

"Then," said the boy, thoughtfully, "I've reached home just in time."

"In time for what?" she asked.

But he did not answer that question. He was thinking of the Demon, and that on the afternoon of this very day he might expect the wise and splendid genius to visit him a second time.

At luncheon, although he did not feel hungry, he joined the family at table and pleased his mother by eating as heartily as of old. He was surprised to find how good the food tasted, and to realize what a pleasure it is to gratify one's sense of taste. The tablets were all right for a journey, he thought, but if he always ate them he would

79

be sure to miss a great deal of enjoyment, since there was no taste to them at all.

At four o'clock he went to his workshop and unlocked the door. Everything was exactly as he had left it, and he looked at his simple electrical devices with some amusement. They seemed tame beside the wonders now in his possession; yet he recollected that his numerous wires had enabled him to strike the Master Key, and therefore should not be despised.

Before long he noticed a quickening in the air, as if it were suddenly surcharged with electric fluid, and the next instant, in a dazzling flash of light, appeared the Demon.

"I am here!" he announced.

"So am I," answered Rob. "But at one time I really thought I should never see you again. I've been—"

"Spare me your history," said the Demon, coldly. "I am aware of your adventures."

80

"Oh, you are!" said Rob, amazed. "Then you know—"

"I know all about your foolish experiences," interrupted the Demon, "for I have been with you constantly, although I remained invisible."

"Then you know what a jolly time I've had," returned the boy. "But why do you call them foolish experiences?"

"Because they were, abominably foolish!" retorted the Demon, bitterly "I entrusted to you gifts of rare scientific interest —electrical devices of such utility that their general adoption by mankind would create a new era in earth life. I hoped your use of these devices would convey such hints to electrical engineers that they would quickly comprehend their mechanism and be able to reproduce them in sufficient quantities to supply the world. And how do you treat these marvelous gifts? Why, you carry them to a cannibal island, where even your crude civilization has not yet penetrated!"

"I wanted to astonish the natives," said Rob, grinning.

The Demon uttered an exclamation of anger, and stamped his foot so fiercely that thousands of electric sparks filled the air, to disappear quickly with a hissing, crinkling sound.

"You might have astonished those ignorant natives as easily by showing them an ordinary electric light," he cried, mockingly. "The power of your gifts would have startled the most advanced electricians of the world. Why did you waste them upon barbarians?"

"Really," faltered Rob, who was frightened and awed by the Demon's vehement anger, "I never intended to visit a cannibal island. I meant to go to Cuba."

"Cuba! Is that a center of advanced scientific thought? Why did you not take your marvels to New York or Chicago; or, if you wished to cross the ocean, to Paris or Vienna?"

"I never thought of those places," acknowledged Rob, meekly.

" Then you were foolish, as I said," declared the Demon, in a calmer tone. "Can you not realize that it is better to be considered great by the intelligent thinkers of the earth, than to be taken for a god by stupid cannibals?"

" Oh, yes, of course," said Rob. "I wish now that I had gone to Europe. But you're not the only one who has a kick coming," he continued. "Your flimsy traveling machine was nearly the death of me."

"Ah, it is true," acknowledged the Demon, frankly. " The case was made of too light material. When the rim was bent it pressed against the works and impeded the proper action of the currents. Had you gone to a civilized country such an accident could not have happened; but to avoid possible trouble in the future I have prepared a new instrument, having a stronger case, which I will exchange for the one you now have."

" That's very kind of you," said Rob, eagerly handing his battered machine to the Demon and receiving the new one in return. "Are you sure this will work?"

" It is impossible for you to injure it," answered the other.

"And how about the next three gifts?" inquired the boy, anxiously.

" Before I grant them," replied the Demon, " you must give me a promise to keep away from uncivilized places and to exhibit your acquirements only among people of intelligence."

"All right," agreed the boy; " I'm not anxious to visit that island again, or any other uncivilized country."

" Then I will add to your possessions three gifts, each more precious and important than the three you have already received."

At this announcement Rob began to

84

quiver with excitement, and sat staring
eagerly at the Demon, while the latter increased in stature and sparkled and glowed
more brilliantly than ever.

CHAPTER EIGHT

ROB ACQUIRES NEW POWERS

"I HAVE seen the folly of sending you into the world with an offensive instrument, yet with no method of defense," resumed the Demon, presently. "You have knocked over a good many people with that tube during the past week."

"I know," said Rob; "but I couldn't help it. It was the only way I had to protect myself."

"Therefore my next gift shall be this Garment of Protection. You must wear it underneath your clothing. It has power to accumulate and exercise electrical repellent force. Perhaps you do not know what that means, so I will explain more fully. When any missile, such as a bullet, sword or lance, approaches your person, its rush through the air will arouse the repellent force of which I speak, and this force, being more powerful than the projective force, will arrest the flight of the missile and throw it back again. Therefore nothing can touch your person that comes with any degree of force or swiftness, and you will be safe from all ordinary weapons. When wearing this Garment you will find it unnecessary to use the electric tube except on rare occasions. Never allow revenge or animosity to influence your conduct. Men may threaten, but they can not injure you, so you must remember that they do not possess your mighty advantages, and that, because of your strength, you should bear with them patiently.''

Rob examined the garment with much curiosity. It glittered like silver, yet was soft and pliable as lamb's wool. Evidently the Demon had prepared it especially for his use, for it was just Rob's size.

"Now," continued the Demon, more gravely, "we approach the subject of an electrical device so truly marvelous that even I am awed when I contemplate the accuracy and perfection of the natural laws which guide it and permit it to exercise its functions. Mankind has as yet conceived nothing like it, for it requires full knowledge of electrical power to understand even its possibilities."

The Being paused, and drew from an inner pocket something resembling a flat metal box. In size it was about four inches by six, and nearly an inch in thickness.

"What is it?" asked Rob, wonderingly.

"It is an automatic Record of Events," answered the Demon.

"I don't understand," said Rob, with hesitation.

" I will explain to you its use," returned

the Demon, "although the electrical forces which operate it and the vibratory currents which are the true records must remain unknown to you until your brain has mastered the higher knowledge of electricity. At present the practical side of this invention will be more interesting to you than a review of its scientific construction.

"Suppose you wish to know the principal events that are occurring in Germany at the present moment. You first turn this little wheel at the side until the word ' GERMANY ' appears in the slot at the small end. Then open the top cover, which is hinged, and those passing events in which you are interested will appear before your eyes. "

The Demon, as he spoke, opened the cover, and, looking within, the boy saw, as in a mirror, a moving picture before him. A regiment of soldiers was marching through the streets of Berlin, and at its head rode a body of horsemen, in the midst of which was the Emperor himself. The people who thronged the sidewalks cheered and waved their hats and handkerchiefs with enthusiasm, while a band of musicians played a German air, which Rob could distinctly hear.

While he gazed, spell-bound, the scene changed, and he looked upon a great warship entering a harbor with flying pennants. The rails were lined with officers and men straining their eyes for the first sight of their beloved "*Vaterland*" after a long foreign cruise, and a ringing cheer, as from a thousand throats, came faintly to Rob's ear.

Again the scene changed, and within a dingy, underground room, hemmed in by walls of stone, and dimly lighted by a flickering lamp, a body of wild-eyed, desperate men were plighting an oath to murder the Emperor and overthrow his government.

"Anarchists?" asked Rob, trembling with excitement.

"Anarchists!" answered the Demon, with

a faint sneer, and he shut the cover of the Record with a sudden snap.

"It's wonderful!" cried the boy, with a sigh that was followed by a slight shiver.

"The Record is, indeed, proof within itself of the marvelous possibilities of electricity. Men are now obliged to depend upon newspapers for information; but these can only relate events long after they have occurred. And newspaper statements are often unreliable and sometimes wholly false, while many events of real importance are never printed in their columns. You may guess what an improvement is this automatic Record of Events, which is as reliable as Truth itself. Nothing can be altered or falsified, for the vibratory currents convey the actual events to your vision, even as they happen."

"But suppose," said Rob, "that something important should happen while I'm asleep, or not looking at the box?"

"I have called this a Record," replied

the Demon, "and such it really is, although I have shown you only such events as are in process of being recorded. By pressing this spring you may open the opposite cover of the box, where all events of importance that have occurred throughout the world during the previous twenty-four hours will appear before you in succession. You may thus study them at your leisure. The various scenes constitute a register of the world's history, and may be recalled to view as often as you desire."

"It's—it's like knowing everything," murmured Rob, deeply impressed for perhaps the first time in his life.

"It *is* knowing everything," returned the Demon; "and this mighty gift I have decided to entrust to your care. Be very careful as to whom you permit to gaze upon these pictures of passing events, for knowledge may often cause great misery to the human race."

"I'll be careful," promised the boy, as

92

he took the box reverently within his own hands.

"The third and last gift of the present series," resumed the Demon, "is one no less curious than the Record of Events, although it has an entirely different value. It is a Character Marker."

"What's that?" inquired Rob.

"I will explain. Perhaps you know that your fellow-creatures are more or less hypocritical. That is, they try to appear good when they are not, and wise when in reality they are foolish. They tell you they are friendly when they positively hate you, and try to make you believe they are kind when their natures are cruel. This hypocrisy seems to be a human failing. One of your writers has said, with truth, that among civilized people things are seldom what they seem."

"I've heard that," remarked Rob.

"On the other hand," continued the Demon, "some people with fierce countenances are kindly by nature, and many who appear to be evil are in reality honorable and trustworthy. Therefore, that you may judge all your fellow-creatures truly, and know upon whom to depend, I give you the Character Marker. It consists of this pair of spectacles. While you wear them every one you meet will be marked upon the forehead with a letter indicating his or her character. The good will bear the letter 'G,' the evil the letter 'E.' The wise will be marked with a 'W' and the foolish with an 'F.' The kind will show a 'K' upon their foreheads and the cruel a letter 'C.' Thus you may determine by a single look the true natures of all those you encounter.''

"And are these, also, electrical in their construction?'' asked the boy, as he took the spectacles.

"Certainly. Goodness, wisdom and kindness are natural forces, creating character. For this reason men are not always to blame for bad character, as they acquire it unconsciously. All character sends out certain electrical vibrations, which these spectacles concentrate in their lenses and exhibit to the gaze of their wearer, as I have explained."

"It's a fine idea," said the boy; "who discovered it?"

"It is a fact that has always existed, but is now utilized for the first time."

"Oh!" said Rob.

"With these gifts, and the ones you acquired a week ago, you are now equipped to astound the world and awaken mankind to a realization of the wonders that may be accomplished by natural forces. See that you employ these powers wisely, in the interests of science, and do not forget your promise to exhibit your electrical marvels only to those who are most capable of comprehending them."

"I'll remember," said Rob.

"Then adieu until a week from to-day,

when I will meet you here at this hour and
bestow upon you the last three gifts which
you are entitled to receive. Good-by!"

"Good-by!" repeated Rob, and in a gorgeous flash of color the Demon disappeared,
leaving the boy alone in the room with his
new and wonderful possessions.

CHAPTER NINE

THE SECOND JOURNEY

BY this time you will have gained a
fair idea of Rob's character. He is,
in truth, a typical American boy, possessing
an average intelligence not yet regulated
by the balance-wheel of experience. The
mysteries of electricity were so attractive
to his eager nature that he had devoted
considerable time and some study to electrical experiment; but his study was the superficial kind that seeks to master only such
details as may be required at the moment.
Moreover, he was full of boyish recklessness and irresponsibility and therefore diffi-

cult to impress with the dignity of science and the gravity of human existence. Life, to him, was a great theater wherein he saw himself the most interesting if not the most important actor, and so enjoyed the play with unbounded enthusiasm.

Aside from the extraordinary accident which had forced the Electrical Demon into his life, Rob may be considered one of those youngsters who might possibly develop into a brilliant manhood or enter upon an ordinary, humdrum existence, as Fate should determine. Just at present he had no thought beyond the passing hour, nor would he bother himself by attempting to look ahead or plan for the future.

Yet the importance of his electrical possessions and the stern injunction of the Demon to use them wisely had rendered the boy more thoughtful than at any previous time during his brief life, and he became so preoccupied at the dinner table that his father and mother cast many anxious looks in his direction.

Of course Rob was anxious to test his newly-acquired powers, and decided to lose no time in starting upon another journey. But he said nothing to any of the family about it, fearing to meet with opposition.

He passed the evening in the sitting-room, in company with his father and mother and sisters, and even controlled his impatience to the extent of playing a game of carom with Nell; but he grew so nervous and impatient at last that his sister gave up the game in disgust and left him to his own amusement.

At one time he thought of putting on the electric spectacles and seeing what the real character of each member of his family might be; but a sudden fear took possession of him that he might regret the act forever afterward. They were his nearest and dearest friends on earth, and in his

boyish heart he loved them all and believed
in their goodness and sincerity. The pos-
sibility of finding a bad character mark on
any of their familiar faces made him shudder, and he determined then and there
never to use the spectacles to view the face
of a friend or relative. Had any one, at
that moment, been gazing at Rob through
the lenses of the wonderful Character
Marker, I am sure a big "W" would have
been found upon the boy's forehead.

When the family circle broke up, and all
retired for the night, Rob kissed his parents
and sisters with real affection before going
to his own room. But, on reaching his
cozy little chamber, instead of preparing
for bed Rob clothed himself in the Garment
of Repulsion. Then he covered the glittering Garment with his best summer suit
of clothes, which effectually concealed it.

He now looked around to see what else
he should take, and thought of an umbrella,
a rain-coat, a book or two to read during

the journey, and several things besides; but he ended by leaving them all behind.

" I can't be loaded down with so much truck," he decided; "and I'm going into civilized countries, this time, where I can get anything I need."

However, to prevent a recurrence of the mistake he had previously made, he tore a map of the world and a map of Europe from his geography, and, folding them up, placed them in his pocket. He also took a small compass that had once been a watch-charm, and, finally, the contents of a small iron bank that opened with a combination lock. This represented all his savings, amounting to two dollars and seventeen cents in dimes, nickles and pennies.

" It isn't a fortune," he thought, as he counted it up, " but I didn't need any money the last trip, so perhaps I'll get along somehow. I don't like to tackle dad for more, for he might ask questions and try to keep me at home."

By the time he had finished his preparations and stowed all his electrical belongings in his various pockets, it was nearly midnight and the house was quiet. So Rob stole down stairs in his stocking feet and noiselessly opened the back door.

It was a beautiful July night and, in addition to the light of the full moon, the sky was filled with the radiance of countless thousands of brilliant stars.

After Rob had put on his shoes he unfolded the map, which was plainly visible by the starlight, and marked the direction he must take to cross the Atlantic and reach London, his first stopping place. Then he consulted his compass, put the indicator of his traveling machine to the word "up," and shot swiftly into the air. When he had reached a sufficient height he placed the indicator to a point north of east and, with a steady and remarkably swift flight, began his journey.

" Here goes," he remarked, with a sense

of exaltation, " for another week of adventure! I wonder what'll happen between
now and next Saturday."

CHAPTER TEN

HOW ROB SERVED A MIGHTY KING

THE new traveling machine was a distinct improvement over the old one, for it carried Rob with wonderful speed across the broad Atlantic.

He fell asleep soon after starting, and only wakened when the sun was high in the heavens. But he found himself whirling along at a good rate, with the greenish shimmer of the peaceful ocean waves spread beneath him far beyond his range of vision.

Being in the track of the ocean steamers it was not long before he found himself overtaking a magnificent vessel whose decks were crowded with passengers. He dropped down some distance, to enable him to see these people more plainly, and while he hovered near he could hear the excited exclamations of the passengers, who focused dozens of marine glasses upon his floating form. This inspection somewhat embarrassed him, and having no mind to be stared at he put on additional speed and soon left the steamer far behind him.

About noon the sky clouded over, and Rob feared a rainstorm was approaching. So he rose to a point considerably beyond the clouds, where the air was thin but remarkably pleasant to inhale and the rays of the sun were not so hot as when reflected by the surface of the water.

He could see the dark clouds rolling beneath him like volumes of smoke from a factory chimney, and knew the earth was catching a severe shower of rain; yet he congratulated himself on his foresight in not being burdened with umbrella or rain-coat, since his elevated position rendered him secure from rain-clouds.

But, having cut himself off from the earth, there remained nothing to see except the clear sky overhead and the tumbling clouds beneath; so he took from his pocket the Automatic Record of Events, and watched with breathless interest the incidents occurring in different parts of the world. A big battle was being fought in the Philippines, and so fiercely was it contested that Rob watched its progress for hours, with rapt attention. Finally a brave rally by the Americans sent their foes to the cover of the woods, where they scattered in every direction, only to form again in a deep valley hidden by high hills.

" If only I was there," thought Rob, " I could show that captain where to find the rebels and capture them. But I guess the Philippines are rather out of my way, so our soldiers will never know how near they are to a complete victory."

The boy also found considerable amusement in watching the course of an insurrec-
tion in Venezuela, where opposing armies
of well-armed men preferred to bluster and
threaten rather than come to blows.

During the evening he found that an
"important event" was Madame Bern-
hardt's production of a new play, and Rob
followed it from beginning to end with great
enjoyment, although he felt a bit guilty at
not having purchased a ticket.

"But it's a crowded house, anyway," he
reflected, "and I'm not taking up a reserved
seat or keeping any one else from seeing the
show. So where's the harm? Yet it seems
to me if these Records get to be common,
as the Demon wishes, people will all stay
at home and see the shows, and the poor
actors 'll starve to death."

The thought made him uneasy, and he
began, for the first time, to entertain a
doubt of the Demon's wisdom in forcing
such devices upon humanity.

The clouds had now passed away and the moon sent her rays to turn the edges of the waves into glistening showers of jewels.

Rob closed the lid of the wonderful Record of Events and soon fell into a deep sleep that held him unconscious for many hours.

When he awoke he gave a start of surprise, for beneath him was land. How long it was since he had left the ocean behind him he could not guess, but his first thought was to set the indicator of the traveling machine to zero and to hover over the country until he could determine where he was.

This was no easy matter. He saw green fields, lakes, groves and villages; but these might exist in any country. Being still at a great elevation he descended gradually until he was about twenty feet from the surface of the earth, where he paused near the edge of a small village.

At once a crowd of excited people assem-

A man rushed toward it, but the next moment he threw
up his hands and fell unconscious

bled, shouting to one another and pointing towards him in wonder. In order to be prepared for emergencies Rob had taken the electric tube from his pocket, and now, as he examined the dress and features of the people below, the tube suddenly slipped from his grasp and fell to the ground, where one end stuck slantingly into the soft earth.

A man rushed eagerly towards it, but the next moment he threw up his hands and fell upon his back, unconscious. Others who ran to assist their fallen comrade quickly tumbled into a heap beside him.

It was evident to Rob that the tube had fallen in such a position that the button was being pressed continually and a current of electric fluid issued to shock whoever came near. Not wishing to injure these people he dropped to the ground and drew the tube from the earth, thus releasing the pressure upon the button.

But the villagers had now decided that the boy was their enemy, and no sooner had he touched the ground than a shower of stones and sticks rained about him. Not one reached his body, however, for the Garment of Repulsion stopped their flight and returned them to rattle with more or less force against those who had thrown them— "like regular boomerangs," thought Rob.

To receive their own blows in this fashion seemed so like magic to the simple folk that with roars of fear and pain they ran away in all directions.

" It's no use stopping here," remarked Rob, regretfully, "for I've spoiled my welcome by this accident. I think these people are Irish, by their looks and speech, so I must be somewhere in the Emerald Isle."

He consulted his map and decided upon the general direction he should take to reach England, after which he again rose into the air and before long was passing over the channel towards the shores of England.

Either his map or compass or his calculations proved wrong, for it was high noon

before, having changed his direction a half
dozen times, he came to the great city of
London. He saw at a glance that it would
never do to drop into the crowded streets,
unless he wanted to become an object of
public curiosity; so he looked around for a
suitable place to alight.

Near by was a monstrous church that
sent a sharp steeple far into the air. Rob
examined this spire and saw a narrow opening in the masonry that led to a small room
where a chime of bells hung. He crept
through the opening and, finding a ladder
that connected the belfry with a platform
below, began to descend.

There were three ladders, and then a
winding flight of narrow, rickety stairs to
be passed before Rob finally reached a
small room in the body of the church. This
room proved to have two doors, one connecting with the auditorium and the other
letting into a side street. Both were
locked, but Rob pointed the electric tube at

the outside door and broke the lock in an instant. Then he walked into the street as composedly as if he had lived all his life in London.

There were plenty of sights to see, you may be sure, and Rob walked around until he was so tired that he was glad to rest upon one of the benches in a beautiful park. Here, half hidden by the trees, he amused himself by looking at the Record of Events.

" London's a great town, and no mistake," he said to himself; " but let's see what the British are doing in South Africa to-day."

He turned the cylinder to "South Africa," and, opening the lid, at once became interested. An English column, commanded by a brave but stubborn officer, was surrounded by the Boer forces and fighting desperately to avoid capture or annihilation.

" This would be interesting to King Edward," thought the boy. " Guess I'll hunt him up and tell him about it."

A few steps away stood a policeman. Rob approached him and asked:

" Where's the king to-day ?"

The officer looked at him with mingled surprise and suspicion.

"'Is Majesty is sojournin' at Marlb'ro 'Ouse, just now," was the reply. "Per'aps you wants to make 'im a wissit," he continued, with lofty sarcasm.

"That's it, exactly," said Rob. "I'm an American, and thought while I was in London I'd drop in on His Royal Highness and say 'hello' to him."

The officer chuckled, as if much amused.

"Hamericans is bloomin' green," he remarked, "so youse can stand for Hamerican, right enough. No other wissitors is such blarsted fools. But yon's the palace, an' I s'pose 'is Majesty'll give ye a 'ot reception."

"Thanks; I'll look him up," said the boy, and left the officer convulsed with laughter,

He soon knew why. The palace was surrounded by a cordon of the king's own life guards, who admitted no one save those who presented proper credentials.

"There's only one thing to do;" thought Rob, " and that's to walk straight in, as I haven't any friends to give me a regular introduction."

So he boldly advanced to the gate, where he found himself stopped by crossed carbines and a cry of "Halt!"

"Excuse me," said Rob; "I'm in a hurry."

He pushed the carbines aside and marched on. The soldiers made thrusts at him with their weapons, and an officer jabbed at his breast with a glittering sword, but the Garment of Repulsion protected him from these dangers as well as from a hail of bullets that followed his advancing figure.

He reached the entrance of the palace only to face another group of guardsmen and a second order to halt, and as these sol-

Rob reached the entrance of the palace, only to face
another group of guardsmen

diers were over six feet tall and stood
shoulder to shoulder Rob saw that he could
not hope to pass them without using his
electric tube.

"Stand aside, you fellows!" he ordered.
There was no response. He extended
the tube and, as he pressed the button, described a semi-circle with the instrument.
Immediately the tall guardsmen toppled
over like so many tenpins, and Rob stepped
across their bodies and penetrated to the reception room, where a brilliant assemblage
awaited, in hushed and anxious groups, foɪ
opportunity to obtain audience with the
king.

"I hope his Majesty isn't busy," said Rob
to a solemn-visaged official who confronted
him. "I want to have a little talk with
him."

"I—I—ah—beg pardon!" exclaimed the
astounded master of ceremonies. "What
name, please?"

"Oh, never mind my name," replied

Rob, and pushing the gentleman aside he entered the audience chamber of the great king.

King Edward was engaged in earnest consultation with one of his ministers, and after a look of surprise in Rob's direction and a grave bow he bestowed no further attention upon the intruder.

But Rob was not to be baffled now.

"Your Majesty," he interrupted, "I've important news for you. A big fight is taking place in South Africa and your soldiers will probably be cut into mince meat."

The minister strode towards the boy angrily.

"Explain this intrusion!" he cried.

"I have explained. The Boers are having a regular killing-bee. Here! take a look at it yourselves."

He drew the Record from his pocket, and at the movement the minister shrank back as if he suspected it was an infernal machine and might blow his head off; but the king stepped quietly to the boy's side and looked into the box when Rob threw open the lid.

As he comprehended the full wonder of the phenomenon he was observing Edward uttered a low cry of amazement, but thereafter he silently gazed upon the fierce battle that still raged far away upon the African *veld*. Before long his keen eye recognized the troops engaged and realized their imminent danger.

"They'll be utterly annihilated!" he gasped. "What shall we do?"

"Oh, we can't do anything just now," answered Rob. "But it's curious to watch how bravely the poor fellows fight for their lives."

The minister, who by this time was also peering into the box, groaned aloud, and then all three forgot their surroundings in the tragedy they were beholding.

Hemmed in by vastly superior numbers, the English were calmly and stub-

bornly resisting every inch of advance and
selling their lives as dearly as possible.
Their leader fell pierced by a hundred bullets, and the king, who had known him
from boyhood, passed his hand across his
eyes as if to shut out the awful sight. But
the fascination of the battle forced him to
look again, and the next moment he cried
aloud:

"Look there! Look there!"

Over the edge of a line of hills appeared
the helmets of a file of English soldiers. They
reached the summit, followed by rank after
rank, until the hillside was alive with them.
And then, with a ringing cheer that came
like a faint echo to the ears of the three
watchers, they broke into a run and dashed
forward to the rescue of their brave comrades. The Boers faltered, gave back, and
the next moment fled precipitately, while
the exhausted survivors of the courageous
band fell sobbing into the arms of their
rescuers.

Rob closed the lid of the Record with a sudden snap that betrayed his deep feeling, and the king pretended to cough behind his handkerchief and stealthily wiped his eyes.

" 'Twasn't so bad, after all," remarked the boy, with assumed cheerfulness; " but it looked mighty ticklish for your men at one time."

King Edward regarded the boy curiously, remembering his abrupt entrance and the marvelous device he had exhibited.

"What do you call that?" he asked, pointing at the Record with a finger that trembled slightly from excitement.

" It is a new electrical invention," replied Rob, replacing it in his pocket, "and so constructed that events are reproduced at the exact moment they occur."

"Where can I purchase one?" demanded the king, eagerly.

"They're not for sale," said Rob. "This one of mine is the first that ever happened."

" Oh !"

"I really think," continued the boy, nodding sagely, "that it wouldn't be well to have these Records scattered around. Their use would give some folks unfair advantage over others, you know."

"Certainly."

"I only showed you this battle because I happened to be in London at the time and thought you'd be interested."

"It was very kind of you," said Edward; "but how did you gain admittance?"

"Well, to tell the truth, I was obliged to knock over a few of your tall life-guards. They seem to think you're a good thing and need looking after, like jam in a cupboard."

The king smiled.

"I hope you haven't killed my guards," said he.

"Oh, no; they'll come around all right."

"It is necessary," continued Edward, "that public men be protected from intrusion, no matter how democratic they may be personally. You would probably find it as difficult to approach the President of the United States as the King of England."

"Oh, I'm not complaining," said Rob. "It wasn't much trouble to break through."

"You seem quite young to have mastered such wonderful secrets of Nature," continued the king.

"So I am," replied Rob, modestly; "but these natural forces have really existed since the beginning of the world, and some one was sure to discover them in time." He was quoting the Demon, although unconsciously.

"You are an American, I suppose," said the minister, coming close to Rob and staring him in the face.

"Guessed right the first time," answered the boy, and drawing his Character Marking spectacles from his pocket, he put them on and stared at the minister in turn.

Upon the man's forehead appeared the letter "E."

"Your Majesty," said Rob, "I have here another queer invention. Will you please wear these spectacles for a few moments?"

The king at once put them on.

"They are called Character Markers," continued the boy, "because the lenses catch and concentrate the character vibrations radiating from every human individual and reflect the true character of the person upon his forehead. If a letter 'G' appears, you may be sure his disposition is good; if his forehead is marked with an 'E' his character is evil, and you must beware of treachery."

The king saw the "E" plainly marked upon his minister's forehead, but he said nothing except "Thank you," and returned the spectacles to Rob.

But the minister, who from the first had been ill at ease, now became positively angry.

"Do not believe him, your Majesty!"

he cried. " It is a trick, and meant to de-
ceive you."

" I did not accuse you," answered the
king, sternly. Then he added: " I wish
to be alone with this young gentleman."

The minister left the room with an anxious face and hanging head.

" Now," said Rob, " let's look over the
record of the past day and see if that fellow
has been up to any mischief."

He turned the cylinder of the Record to
" England," and slowly the events of the
last twenty-four hours were reproduced,
one after the other, upon the polished plate.

Before long the king uttered an exclamation. The Record pictured a small room
in which were seated three gentlemen engaged in earnest conversation. One of them
was the accused minister.

" Those men," said the king in a low
voice, while he pointed out the other two,
"are my avowed enemies. This is proof that
your wonderful spectacles indicated my min-

ister's character with perfect truth. I am grateful to you for thus putting me upon my guard, for I have trusted the man fully."

"Oh, don't mention it," replied the boy, lightly; "I'm glad to have been of service to you. But it's time for me to go."

"I hope you will favor me with another interview," said the king, "for I am much interested in your electrical inventions. I will instruct my guards to admit you at any time, so you will not be obliged to fight your way in."

"All right. But it really doesn't matter," answered Rob. "It's no trouble at all to knock 'em over."

Then he remembered his manners and bowed low before the king, who seemed to him "a fine fellow and not a bit stuck up." And then he walked calmly from the palace.

The people in the outer room stared at him wonderingly and the officer of the guard saluted the boy respectfully. But Rob only smiled in an amused way as he marched past them with his hands thrust deep into his trousers' pockets and his straw hat tipped jauntily upon the back of his head.

CHAPTER ELEVEN

THE MAN OF SCIENCE

R OB passed the remainder of the day
wandering about London and amusing himself by watching the peculiar ways
of the people. When it became so dark
that there was no danger of his being observed, he rose through the air to the narrow slit in the church tower and lay upon
the floor of the little room, with the bells
hanging all around him, to pass the night.

He was just falling asleep when a tremendous din and clatter nearly deafened
him, and set the whole tower trembling.
It was the midnight chime.

Rob clutched his ears tightly, and when
the vibrations had died away descended by
the ladder to a lower platform. But even
here the next hourly chime made his ears
ring, and he kept descending from platform
to platform until the last half of a restless
night was passed in the little room at the
bottom of the tower.

When, at daylight, the boy sat up
and rubbed his eyes, he said, wearily:
" Churches are all right as churches; but
as hotels they are rank failures. I ought to
have bunked in with my friend, King Edward."

He climbed up the stairs and the ladders
again and looked out the little window in
the belfry. Then he examined his map
of Europe.

" I believe I'll take a run over to Paris,"
he thought. " I must be home again by
Saturday, to meet the Demon, so I'll have
to make every day count."

Without waiting for breakfast, since he

had eaten a tablet the evening before, he crept through the window and mounted into the fresh morning air until the great city with its broad waterway lay spread out beneath him. Then he sped away to the southeast and, crossing the channel, passed between Amiens and Rouen and reached Paris before ten o'clock.

Near the outskirts of the city appeared a high tower, upon the flat roof of which a man was engaged in adjusting a telescope. Upon seeing Rob, who was passing at no great distance from this tower, the man cried out:

"*Approchez!—Venez ici!*"

Then he waved his hands frantically in the air, and fairly danced with excitement. So the boy laughed and dropped down to the roof where, standing beside the Frenchman, whose eyes were actually protruding from their sockets, he asked, coolly:

"Well, what do you want?"

The other was for a moment speechless.

The eyes of the Frenchman were actually protruding
from their sockets

He was a tall, lean man, having a bald head but a thick, iron-gray beard, and his black eyes sparkled brightly from behind a pair of gold-rimmed spectacles. After attentively regarding the boy for a time he said, in broken English:

"But, M'sieur, how can you fly wizout ze —ze machine? I have experiment myself wiz some air-ship; but you—zere is nossing to make go!"

Rob guessed that here was his opportunity to do the Demon a favor by explaining his electrical devices to this new acquaintance, who was evidently a man of science.

"Here is the secret, Professor," he said, and holding out his wrist displayed the traveling machine and explained, as well as he could, the forces that operated it.

The Frenchman, as you may suppose, was greatly astonished, and to show how perfectly the machine worked Rob turned the indicator and rose a short distance above the tower, circling around it before he re-

joined the professor on the roof. Then he
showed his food tablets, explaining how
each was stored with sufficient nourishment
for an entire day.

The scientist positively gasped for breath,
so powerful was the excitement he experienced at witnessing these marvels.

"Eet is wonderful—grand—magnifique!"
he exclaimed.

"But here is something of still greater
interest," continued Rob, and taking the
Automatic Record of Events from his pocket
he allowed the professor to view the remarkable scenes that were being enacted
throughout the civilized world.

The Frenchman was now trembling violently, and he implored Rob to tell him
where he might obtain similar electrical machines.

"I can't do that," replied the boy, decid-
edly; "but, having seen these, you may be
able to discover their construction for yourself. Now that you know such things to be

possible and practical, the hint should be sufficient to enable a shrewd electrician to prepare duplicates of them."

The scientist glared at him with evident disappointment, and Rob continued:

"These are not all the wonders I can exhibit. Here is another electrical device that is, perhaps, the most remarkable of any I possess."

He took the Character Marking spectacles from his pocket and fitted them to his eyes. Then he gave a whistle of surprise and turned his back upon his new friend. He had seen upon the Frenchman's forehead the letters "E" and "C."

" Guess I've struck the wrong sort of scientist, after all!" he muttered, in a disgusted tone.

His companion was quick to prove the accuracy of the Character Marker. Seeing the boy's back turned, he seized a long iron bar that was used to operate the telescope, and struck at Rob so fiercely that had he not worn the Garment of Protection his skull would have been crushed by the blow. As it was, the bar rebounded with a force that sent the murderous Frenchman sprawling upon the roof, and Rob turned around and laughed at him.

"It won't work, Professor," he said. "I'm proof against assassins. Perhaps you had an idea that when you had killed me you could rob me of my valuable possessions; but they wouldn't be a particle of use to a scoundrel like you, I assure you! Good morning."

Before the surprised and baffled scientist could collect himself sufficiently to reply, the boy was soaring far above his head and searching for a convenient place to alight, that he might investigate the charms of this famed city of Paris.

It was indeed a beautiful place, with many stately buildings lining the shady boulevards. So thronged were the streets that Rob well knew he would soon be the center of a curious crowd should he alight upon them. Already a few sky-gazers had noted the boy moving high in the air, above their heads, and one or two groups stood pointing their fingers at him.

Pausing at length above the imposing structure of the Hotel Anglais, Rob noticed at one of the upper floors an open window, before which was a small iron balcony. Alighting upon this he proceeded to enter, without hesitation, the open window. He heard a shriek and a cry of "*Au voleur!*" and caught sight of a woman's figure as she dashed into an adjoining room, slamming and locking the door behind her.

"I don't know as I blame her," observed Rob, with a smile at the panic he had created. "I s'pose she takes me for a burglar, and thinks I've climbed up the lightning rod."

He soon found the door leading into the

hallway and walked down several flights of stairs until he reached the office of the hotel.

" How much do you charge a day?" he inquired, addressing a fat and pompous-looking gentleman behind the desk.

The man looked at him in a surprised way, for he had not heard the boy enter the room. But he said something in French to a waiter who was passing, and the latter came to Rob and made a low bow.

" I speak ze Eengliss ver' fine," he said. "What desire have you?"

" What are your rates by the day?" asked the boy.

" Ten francs, M'sieur."

" How many dollars is that?"

"Dollar Americaine?"

"Yes; United States money."

"Ah, *oui!* Eet is ze two dollar, M'sieur."

"All right; I can stay about a day before I go bankrupt. Give me a room."

"*Certainement*, M'sieur. Have you ze luggage?"

"No; but I'll pay in advance," said Rob, and began counting out his dimes and nickles and pennies, to the unbounded amazement of the waiter, who looked as if he had never seen such coins before.

He carried the money to the fat gentleman, who examined the pieces curiously, and there was a long conference between them before it was decided to accept them in payment for a room for a day. But at this season the hotel was almost empty, and when Rob protested that he had no other money the fat gentleman put the coins into his cash box with a resigned sigh and the waiter showed the boy to a little room at the very top of the building.

Rob washed and brushed the dust from his clothes, after which he sat down and amused himself by viewing the pictures that constantly formed upon the polished plate of the Record of Events.

CHAPTER TWELVE

HOW ROB SAVED A REPUBLIC

WHILE following the shifting scenes of the fascinating Record Rob noted an occurrence that caused him to give a low whistle of astonishment and devote several moments to serious thought.

"I believe it's about time I interfered with the politics of this Republic," he said, at last, as he closed the lid of the metal box and restored it to his pocket. "If I don't take a hand there probably won't be a Republic of France very long and, as a good American, I prefer a republic to a monarchy."

Then he walked down-stairs and found his English-speaking waiter.

"Where's President Loubet?" he asked.

"Ze President! Ah, he is wiz his mansion. To be at his residence, M'sieur."

"Where is his residence?"

The waiter began a series of voluble and explicit directions which so confused the boy that he exclaimed:

"Oh, much obliged!" and walked away in disgust.

Gaining the street he approached a gendarme and repeated his question, with no better result than before, for the fellow waved his arms wildly in all directions and roared a volley of incomprehensible French phrases that conveyed no meaning whatever.

"If ever I travel in foreign countries again," said Rob, "I'll learn their lingo in advance. Why doesn't the Demon get up a conversation machine that will speak all languages?"

By dint of much inquiry, however, and after walking several miles following ambiguous directions, he managed to reach the residence of President Loubet. But there he was politely informed that the President was busily engaged in his garden, and would see no one.

"That's all right," said the boy, calmly. "If he's in the garden I'll have no trouble finding him."

Then, to the amazement of the Frenchmen, Rob shot into the air fifty feet or so, from which elevation he overlooked a pretty garden in the rear of the President's mansion. The place was protected from ordinary intrusion by high walls, but Rob descended within the enclosure and walked up to a man who was writing at a small table placed under the spreading branches of a large tree.

"Is this President Loubet?" he inquired, with a bow.

The gentleman looked up.

"My servants were instructed to allow no one to disturb me," he said, speaking in excellent English.

"It isn't their fault; I flew over the wall," returned Rob. "The fact is," he added, hastily, as he noted the President's frown, "I have come to save the Republic; and I haven't much time to waste over a bundle of Frenchmen, either."

The President seemed surprised.

"Your name!" he demanded, sharply.

"Robert Billings Joslyn, United States of America!"

"Your business, Monsieur Joslyn!"

Rob drew the Record from his pocket and placed it upon the table.

"This, sir," said he, "is an electrical device that records all important events. I wish to call your attention to a scene enacted in Paris last evening which may have an effect upon the future history of your country."

He opened the lid, placed the Record so

139

that the President could see clearly, and
then watched the changing expressions
upon the great man's face; first indifference,
then interest, the next moment eagerness
and amazement.

"*Mon Dieu!*" he gasped; " the Orlean-
ists!"

Rob nodded.

" Yes; they've worked up a rather pretty
plot, haven't they?"

The President did not reply. He was
anxiously watching the Record and scrib-
bling notes on a paper beside him. His
face was pale and his lips tightly compressed.

Finally he leaned back in his chair and
asked :

"Can you reproduce this scene again?"

"Certainly, sir," answered the boy; "as
often as you like."

"Will you remain here while I send for
my minister of police? It will require but a
short time."

"Call him up, then. I'm in something

Rob watched the changing expressions upon the
great man's face

of a hurry myself, but now I've mixed up with this thing I'll see it through.''

The President touched a bell and gave an order to his servant. Then he turned to Rob and said, wonderingly:

"You are a boy!''

"That's true, Mr. President," was the answer; "but an American boy, you must remember. That makes a big difference, I assure you.''

The President bowed gravely.

"This is your invention?'' he asked.

"No; I'm hardly equal to that. But the inventor has made me a present of the Record, and it's the only one in the world.''

" It is a marvel,'' remarked the President, thoughtfully. " More! It is a real miracle. We are living in an age of wonders, my young friend.''

" No one knows that better than myself, sir,'' replied Rob. " But, tell me, can you trust your chief of police?''

" I think so,'' said the President, slowly;

"yet since your invention has shown me that many men I have considered honest are criminally implicated in this royalist plot, I hardly know whom to depend upon."

"Then please wear these spectacles during your interview with the minister of police," said the boy. "You must say nothing, while he is with us, about certain marks that will appear upon his forehead; but when he has gone I will explain those marks so you will understand them."

The President covered his eyes with the spectacles.

"Why," he exclaimed, "I see upon your own brow the letters—"

"Stop, sir!" interrupted Rob, with a blush; "I don't care to know what the letters are, if it's just the same to you."

The President seemed puzzled by this speech, but fortunately the minister of police arrived just then and, under Rob's guidance, the pictured record of the Orleanist plot was reproduced before the startled eyes of the official.

"And now," said the boy, " let us see if any of this foolishness is going on just at present."

He turned to the opposite side of the Record and allowed the President and his minister of police to witness the quick succession of events even as they occurred.

Suddenly the minister cried, " Ha!" and, pointing to the figure of a man disembarking from an English boat at Calais, he said, excitedly:

" That, your Excellency, is the Duke of Orleans, in disguise! I must leave you for a time, that I may issue some necessary orders to my men; but this evening I shall call to confer with you regarding the best mode of suppressing this terrible plot."

When the official had departed, the President removed the spectacles from his eyes and handed them to Rob.

" What did you see ?" asked the boy.

" The letters 'G' and 'W'."

" Then you may trust him fully," declared Rob, and explained the construction of the Character Marker to the interested and amazed statesman.

"And now I must go," he continued, " for my stay in your city will be a short one and I want to see all I can."

The President scrawled something on a sheet of paper and signed his name to it, afterward presenting it, with a courteous bow, to his visitor.

" This will enable you to go wherever you please, while in Paris," he said. "I regret my inability to reward you properly for the great service you have rendered my country; but you have my sincerest gratitude, and may command me in any way."

" Oh, that's all right," answered Rob. " I thought it was my duty to warn you, and if you look sharp you'll be able to break up this conspiracy. But I don't want any reward. Good day, sir."

He turned the indicator of his traveling machine and immediately rose into the air, followed by a startled exclamation from the President of France.

Moving leisurely over the city, he selected a deserted thoroughfare to alight in, from whence he wandered unobserved into the beautiful boulevards. These were now brilliantly lighted, and crowds of pleasure seekers thronged them everywhere. Rob experienced a decided sense of relief as he mixed with the gay populace and enjoyed the sights of the splendid city, for it enabled him to forget, for a time, the responsibilities thrust upon him by the possession of the Demon's marvelous electrical devices.

CHAPTER THIRTEEN

ROB LOSES HIS TREASURES

OUR young adventurer had intended to pass the night in the little bed at his hotel, but the atmosphere of Paris proved so hot and disagreeable that he decided it would be more enjoyable to sleep while journeying through the cooler air that lay far above the earth's surface. So just as the clocks were striking the midnight hour Rob mounted skyward and turned the indicator of the traveling machine to the east, intending to make the city of Vienna his next stop.

He had risen to a considerable distance,

where the air was remarkably fresh and exhilarating, and the relief he experienced from the close and muggy streets of Paris was of such a soothing nature that he presently fell fast asleep. His day in the metropolis had been a busy one, for, like all boys, he had forgotten himself in the delight of sight-seeing and had tired his muscles and exhausted his strength to an unusual degree.

It was about three o'clock in the morning when Rob, moving restlessly in his sleep, accidently touched with his right hand the indicator of the machine which was fastened to his left wrist, setting it a couple of points to the south of east. He was, of course, unaware of the slight alteration in his course, which was destined to prove of serious importance in the near future. For the boy's fatigue induced him to sleep far beyond daybreak, and during this period of unconsciousness he was passing over the face of European countries and approaching

147

the lawless and dangerous dominions of the Orient.

When, at last, he opened his eyes, he was puzzled to determine where he was. Beneath him stretched a vast, sandy plain, and speeding across this he came to a land abounding in luxuriant vegetation.

The centrifugal force which propelled him was evidently, for some reason, greatly accelerated, for the scenery of the country he was crossing glided by him at so rapid a rate of speed that it nearly took his breath away.

"I wonder if I've passed Vienna in the night," he thought. "It ought not to have taken me more than a few hours to reach there from Paris."

Vienna was at that moment fifteen hundred miles behind him; but Rob's geography had always been his stumbling block at school, and he had not learned to gage the speed of the traveling machine; so he was completely mystified as to his whereabouts.

Presently a village having many queer spires and minarets whisked by him like a flash. Rob became worried, and resolved to slow up at the next sign of habitation.

This was a good resolution, but Turkestan is so thinly settled that before the boy could plan out a course of action he had passed the barren mountain range of Thian-Shan as nimbly as an acrobat leaps a jumping-bar.

"This won't do at all!" he exclaimed, earnestly. "The traveling machine seems to be running away with me, and I'm missing no end of sights by scooting along up here in the clouds."

He turned the indicator to zero, and was relieved to find it obey with customary quickness. In a few moments he had slowed up and stopped, when he found himself suspended above another stretch of sandy plain. Being too high to see the surface of the plain distinctly he dropped down a few hundred feet to a lower level, where he discovered he was surrounded by billows of sand as far as his eye could reach.

"It's a desert, all right," was his comment; "perhaps old Sahara herself."

He started the machine again towards the east, and at a more moderate rate of speed skimmed over the surface of the desert. Before long he noticed a dark spot ahead of him which proved to be a large body of fierce looking men, riding upon dromedaries and slender, spirited horses and armed with long rifles and crookedly shaped simitars.

"Those fellows seem to be looking for trouble," remarked the boy, as he glided over them, "and it wouldn't be exactly healthy for an enemy to get in their way. But I haven't time to stop, so I'm not likely to get mixed up in any rumpus with them."

" Those fellows seem to be looking for trouble "

However, the armed caravan was scarcely out of sight before Rob discovered he was approaching a rich, wooded oasis of the desert, in the midst of which was built the walled city of Yarkand. Not that he had ever heard of the place, or knew its name; for few Europeans and only one American traveler had ever visited it. But he guessed it was a city of some importance from its size and beauty, and resolved to make a stop there.

Above the high walls projected many slender, white minarets, indicating that the inhabitants were either Turks or some race of Mohammedans; so Rob decided to make investigations before trusting himself to their company.

A cluster of tall trees with leafy tops stood a short distance outside the walls, and here the boy landed and sat down to rest in the refreshing shade.

The city seemed as hushed and still as if it were deserted, and before him stretched the vast plain of white, heated sands. He strained his eyes to catch a glimpse of the band of warriors he had passed, but they were moving slowly and had not yet appeared.

The trees that sheltered Rob were the only ones without the city, although many low bushes or shrubs grew scattering over the space between him and the walls. An arched gateway broke the enclosure at his left, but the gates were tightly shut.

Something in the stillness and the intense heat of the mid-day sun made the boy drowsy. He stretched himself upon the ground beneath the dense foliage of the biggest tree and abandoned himself to the languor that was creeping over him.

" I'll wait until that army of the desert arrives," he thought, sleepily. " They either belong in this city or have come to capture it, so I can tell better what to dance when I find out what the band plays."

The next moment he was sound asleep,

sprawling upon his back in the shade and slumbering as peacefully as an infant.

And while he lay motionless three men dropped in quick succession from the top of the city wall and hid among the low bushes, crawling noiselessly from one to another and so approaching, by degrees, the little group of trees.

They were Turks, and had been sent by those in authority within the city to climb the tallest tree of the group and discover if the enemy was near. For Rob's conjecture had been correct, and the city of Yarkand awaited, with more or less anxiety, a threatened assault from its hereditary enemies, the Tatars.

The three spies were not less forbidding in appearance than the horde of warriors Rob had passed upon the desert. Their features were coarse and swarthy, and their eyes had a most villainous glare. Old fashioned pistols and double-edged daggers were stuck in their belts and their clothing, though of gorgeous colors, was soiled and neglected.

With all the caution of the American savage these Turks approached the tree, where, to their unbounded amazement, they saw the boy lying asleep. His dress and fairness of skin at once proclaimed him, in their shrewd eyes, a European, and their first thought was to glance around in search of his horse or dromedary. Seeing nothing of the kind near they were much puzzled to account for his presence, and stood looking down at him with evident curiosity.

The sun struck the polished surface of the traveling machine which was attached to Rob's wrist and made the metal glitter like silver. This attracted the eyes of the tallest Turk, who stooped down and stealthily unclasped the band of the machine from the boy's outstretched arm. Then, after a hurried but puzzled examination of the little instrument, he slipped it into the pocket of his jacket.

Rob stirred uneasily in his sleep, and one of the Turks drew a slight but stout rope from his breast and with gentle but deft movement passed it around the boy's wrists and drew them together behind him. The action was not swift enough to arouse the power of repulsion in the Garment of Protection, but it awakened Rob effectually, so that he sat up and stared hard at his captors.

"What are you trying to do, anyhow?" he demanded.

The Turks laughed and said something in their own language. They had no knowledge of English.

"You're only making fools of yourselves," continued the boy, wrathfully. "It's impossible for you to injure me."

The three paid no attention to his words. One of them thrust his hand into Rob's pocket and drew out the electric tube. His ignorance of modern appliances was so great that he did not know enough to push the

button. Rob saw him looking down the
hollow end of the tube and murmured:

"I wish it would blow your ugly head
off!"

But the fellow, thinking the shining metal
might be of some value to him, put the tube
in his own pocket and then took from the
prisoner the silver box of tablets.

Rob writhed and groaned at losing his
possessions in this way, and while his hands
were fastened behind him tried to feel for
and touch the indicator of the traveling machine. When he found that the machine
also had been taken, his anger gave way to
fear, for he realized he was in a dangerously
helpless condition.

The third Turk now drew the Record of
Events from the boy's inner pocket. He
knew nothing of the springs that opened
the lids, so, after a curious glance at it, he
secreted the box in the folds of his sash and
continued the search of the captive. The
Character Marking Spectacles were next ab-

stracted, but the Turk, seeing in them nothing but spectacles, scornfully thrust them
back into Rob's pocket, while his comrades
laughed at him. The boy was now rifled
of seventeen cents in pennies, a broken
pocket knife and a lead-pencil, the last article seeming to be highly prized.

After they had secured all the booty they
could find, the tall Turk, who seemed the
leader of the three, violently kicked at
the prisoner with his heavy boot. His surprise was great when the Garment of Repulsion arrested the blow and nearly over-
threw the aggressor in turn. Snatching a
dagger from his sash, he bounded upon the
boy so fiercely that the next instant the en-
raged Turk found himself lying upon his
back three yards away, while his dagger
flew through the air and landed deep in the
desert sands.

" Keep it up !" cried Rob, bitterly. " I
hope you'll enjoy yourself."

The other Turks raised their comrade to

his feet, and the three stared at one another in surprise, being unable to understand how a bound prisoner could so effectually defend himself. But at a whispered word from the leader, they drew their long pistols and fired point blank into Rob's face. The volley echoed sharply from the city walls, but as the smoke drifted slowly away the Turks were horrified to see their intended victim laughing at them.

Uttering cries of terror and dismay, the three took to their heels and bounded towards the wall, where a gate quickly opened to receive them, the populace feeling sure the Tatar horde was upon them.

Nor was this guess so very far wrong; for as Rob, sitting disconsolate upon the sand, raised his eyes, he saw across the desert a dark line that marked the approach of the invaders.

Nearer and nearer they came, while Rob watched them and bemoaned the foolish impulse that had led him to fall asleep in an

Uttering cries of terror and dismay, the three Turks
took to their heels

unknown land where he could so easily be overpowered and robbed of his treasures.

" I always suspected these electrical inventions would be my ruin some day," he reflected, sadly; " and now I'm side-tracked and left helpless in this outlandish country, without a single hope of ever getting home again. They probably won't be able to kill me, unless they find my Garment of Repulsion and strip that off; but I never could cross this terrible desert on foot and, having lost my food tablets, I'd soon starve if I attempted it."

Fortunately, he had eaten one of the tablets just before going to sleep, so there was no danger of immediate starvation. But he was miserable and unhappy, and remained brooding over his cruel fate until a sudden shout caused him to look up.

CHAPTER FOURTEEN

TURK AND TATAR

THE Tatars had arrived, swiftly and noiselessly, and a dozen of the warriors, still mounted, were surrounding him.

His helpless condition aroused their curiosity, and while some of them hastily cut away his bonds and raised him to his feet, others plied him with questions in their own language. Rob shook his head to indicate that he could not understand; so they led him to the chief—an immense, bearded representative of the tribe of Kara-Khitai, the terrible and relentless Black Tatars of Thibet. The huge frame of this fellow was clothed in flowing robes of cloth-of-gold, braided with jewels, and he sat majestically upon the back of a jet-black camel.

Under ordinary circumstances the stern features and flashing black eyes of this redoubtable warrior would have struck a chill of fear to the boy's heart; but now under the influence of the crushing misfortunes he had experienced, he was able to gaze with indifference upon the terrible visage of the desert chief.

The Tatar seemed not to consider Rob an enemy. Instead, he looked upon him as an ally, since the Turks had bound and robbed him.

Finding it impossible to converse with the chief, Rob took refuge in the sign language. He turned his pockets wrong side out, showed the red welts left upon his wrists by the tight cord, and then shook his fists angrily in the direction of the town.

In return the Tatar nodded gravely and issued an order to his men.

By this time the warriors were busily pitching tents before the walls of Yarkand and making preparations for a formal siege. In obedience to the chieftain's orders, Rob was given a place within one of the tents nearest the wall and supplied with a brace of brass-mounted pistols and a dagger with a sharp, zigzag edge. These were evidently to assist the boy in fighting the Turks, and he was well pleased to have them. His spirits rose considerably when he found he had fallen among friends, although most of his new comrades had such evil faces that it was unnecessary to put on the Character Markers to judge their natures with a fair degree of accuracy.

" I can't be very particular about the company I keep," he thought, " and this gang hasn't tried to murder me, as the rascally Turks did. So for the present I'll stand in with the scowling chief and try to get a shot at the thieves who robbed me. If our side wins I may get a chance to recover some of my property. It's a slim chance, of course, but it's the only hope I have left."

That very evening an opportunity occurred for Rob to win glory in the eyes of his new friends. Just before sundown the gates of the city flew open and a swarm of Turks, mounted upon fleet horses and camels, issued forth and fell upon their enemies. The Tatars, who did not expect the sally, were scarcely able to form an opposing rank when they found themselves engaged in a hand-to-hand conflict, fighting desperately for their lives. In such a battle, however, the Turks were at a disadvantage, for the active Tatars slipped beneath their horses and disabled them, bringing both the animals and their riders to the earth.

At the first onslaught Rob shot his pistol at a Turk and wounded him so severely that he fell from his horse. Instantly the boy seized the bridle and sprang upon the steed's back, and the next moment he had dashed into the thickest part of the fray. Bullets and blows rained upon him from all sides, but the Garment of Repulsion saved him from a single scratch.

When his pistols had been discharged he caught up the broken handle of a spear, and used it as a club, galloping into the ranks of the Turks and belaboring them as hard as he could. The Tatars cheered and followed him, and the Turks were so amazed at his miraculous escape from their bullets that they became terrified, thinking he bore a charmed life and was protected by unseen powers.

This terror helped turn the tide of battle, and before long the enemy was pressed back to the walls and retreated through the gates, which were hastily fastened behind them.

In order to prevent a repetition of this sally the Tatars at once invested the gates, so that if the Turks should open them they were as likely to let their foes in as to oppose them.

While the tents were being moved up Rob had an opportunity to search the battlefield for the bodies of the three Turks who had robbed him, but they were not among the fallen.

"Those fellows were too cowardly to take part in a fair fight," declared the boy; but he was much disappointed, nevertheless, as he felt very helpless without the electric tube or the traveling machine.

The Tatar chief now called Rob to his tent and presented him with a beautiful ring set with a glowing pigeon's-blood ruby, in acknowledgment of his services. This gift made the boy feel very proud, and he said to the chief:

"You're all right, old man, even if you do look like a pirate. If you can manage to capture that city, so I can get my electrical devices back, I'll consider you a trump as long as I live."

The chief thought this speech was intended to express Rob's gratitude, so he bowed solemnly in return.

During the night that followed upon the first engagement of the Turks and Tatars, the boy lay awake trying to devise some plan to capture the city. The walls seemed too high and thick to be either scaled or broken by the Tatars, who had no artillery whatever; and within the walls lay all the fertile part of the oasis, giving the besieged a good supply of water and provisions, while the besiegers were obliged to subsist on what water and food they had brought with them.

Just before dawn Rob left his tent and went out to look at the great wall. The stars gave plenty of light, but the boy was worried to find that, according to Eastern custom, no sentries or guards whatever had been posted and all the Tatars were slumbering soundly.

The city was likewise wrapped in profound silence, but just as Rob was turning away he saw a head project stealthily over the edge of the wall before him, and recognized in the features one of the Turks who had robbed him.

Finding no one awake except the boy the fellow sat upon the edge of the wall, with his feet dangling downward, and grinned wickedly at his former victim. Rob watched him with almost breathless eagerness.

After making many motions that conveyed no meaning whatever, the Turk drew the electric tube from his pocket and pointed his finger first at the boy and then at the instrument, as if inquiring what it was used for. Rob shook his head. The Turk turned the tube over several times and examined it carefully, after which he also shook his head, seeming greatly puzzled.

By this time the boy was fairly trembling with excitement. He longed to recover this

valuable weapon, and feared that at any
moment the curious Turk would discover its
use. He held out his hand toward the tube,
and tried to say, by motions, that he would
show the fellow how to use it. The man
seemed to understand, but he would not let
the glittering instrument out of his possession.

Rob was almost in despair, when he happened to notice upon his hand the ruby ring
given him by the chief. Drawing the jewel
from his finger he made offer, by signs, that
he would exchange it for the tube.

The Turk was much pleased with the
idea, and nodded his head repeatedly, holding out his hand for the ring. Rob had little confidence in the man's honor, but he
was so eager to regain the tube that he decided to trust him. So he threw the ring to
the top of the wall, where the Turk caught
it skilfully; but when Rob held out his hand
for the tube the scoundrel only laughed at
him and began to scramble to his feet in or-

der to beat a retreat. Chance, however, foiled this disgraceful treachery, for in his hurry the Turk allowed the tube to slip from his grasp, and it rolled off the wall and fell upon the sand at Rob's very feet.

The robber turned to watch its fall and, filled with sudden anger, the boy grabbed the weapon, pointed it at his enemy, and pressed the button. Down tumbled the Turk, without a cry, and lay motionless at the foot of the wall.

Rob's first thought was to search the pockets of his captive, and to his delight he found and recovered his box of food tablets. The Record of Events and the traveling machine were doubtless in the possession of the other robbers, but Rob did not despair of recovering them, now that he had the tube to aid him.

Day was now breaking, and several of the Tatars appeared and examined the body of the Turk with grunts of surprise, for there was no mark upon him to show how he had been slain. Supposing him to be dead, they tossed him aside and forgot all about him.

Rob had secured his ruby ring again, and going to the chief's tent he showed the jewel to the guard and was at once admitted. The black-bearded chieftain was still reclining upon his pillows, but Rob bowed before him, and by means of signs managed to ask for a band of warriors to assist him in assaulting the town. The chieftain appeared to doubt the wisdom of the enterprise, not being able to understand how the boy could expect to succeed; but he graciously issued the required order, and by the time Rob reached the city gate he found a large group of Tatars gathered to support him, while the entire camp, roused to interest in the proceedings, stood looking on.

Rob cared little for the quarrel between the Turks and Tatars, and under ordinary circumstances would have refused to side with one or the other; but he knew he could not hope to recover his electrical machines

unless the city was taken by the band of warriors who had befriended him, so he determined to force an entrance for them.

Without hesitation he walked close to the
great gate and shattered its fastenings with
the force of the electric current directed
upon them from the tube. Then, shouting
to his friends the Tatars for assistance, they
rushed in a body upon the gate and dashed
it open.

The Turks had expected trouble when
they heard the fastenings of the huge gate
splinter and fall apart, so they had assembled
in force before the opening. As the Tatars
poured through the gateway in a compact
mass they were met by a hail of bullets,
spears and arrows, which did fearful execu-
tion among them. Many were killed outright, while others fell wounded to be tram-
pled upon by those who pressed on from
the rear.

Rob maintained his position in the front
rank, but escaped all injury through the

possession of the Garment of Repulsion. But he took an active part in the fight and pressed the button of the electric tube again and again, tumbling the enemy into heaps on every side, even the horses and camels falling helplessly before the resistless current of electricity.

The Tatars shouted joyfully as they witnessed this marvelous feat and rushed forward to assist in the slaughter; but the boy motioned them all back. He did not wish any more bloodshed than was necessary, and knew that the heaps of unconscious Turks around him would soon recover.

So he stood alone and faced the enemy, calmly knocking them over as fast as they came near. Two of the Turks managed to creep up behind the boy, and one of them, who wielded an immense simitar with a two-edged blade as sharp as a razor, swung the weapon fiercely to cut off Rob's head. But the repulsive force aroused in the Garment was so terrific that it sent the weapon flying backwards with redoubled swiftness, so that it caught the second Turk at the waist and cut him fairly in two.

Thereafter they all avoided coming near the boy, and in a surprisingly short time the Turkish forces were entirely conquered, all having been reduced to unconsciousness except a few cowards who had run away and hidden in the cellars or garrets of the houses.

The Tatars entered the city with shouts of triumph, and the chief was so delighted that he threw his arms around Rob's neck and embraced him warmly.

Then began the sack of Yarkand, the fierce Tatars plundering the bazaars and houses, stripping them of everything of value they could find.

Rob searched anxiously among the bodies of the unconscious Turks for the two men who had robbed him, but neither could be found. He was more successful later, for in running through the streets he came upon a band of Tatars leading a man with a rope around his neck, whom Rob quickly recognized as one of the thieves he was hunting for. The Tatars willingly allowed him to search the fellow, and in one of his pockets Rob found the Record of Events.

He had now recovered all his property, except the traveling machine, the one thing that was absolutely necessary to enable him to escape from this barbarous country.

He continued his search persistently, and an hour later found the dead body of the third robber lying in the square in the center of the city. But the traveling machine was not on his person, and for the first time the boy began to give way to despair.

In the distance he heard loud shouts and sound of renewed strife, warning him that the Turks were recovering consciousness and engaging the Tatars with great fierceness. The latter had scattered throughout the town, thinking themselves perfectly secure, so that not only were they unprepared to fight, but they became panic-stricken at seeing their foes return, as it seemed, from death to life. Their usual courage forsook them, and they ran, terrified, in every direction, only to be cut down by the revengeful Turkish simitars.

Rob was sitting upon the edge of a marble fountain in the center of the square when a crowd of victorious Turks appeared and quickly surrounded him. The boy paid no attention to their gestures and the Turks feared to approach him nearly, so they stood a short distance away and fired volleys at him from their rifles and pistols.

Rob glared at them scornfully, and seeing they could not injure him the Turks desisted; but they still surrounded him, and the crowd grew thicker every moment.

Women now came creeping from their hiding places and mingled with the ranks of the men, and Rob guessed, from their joyous chattering, that the Turks had regained the city and driven out or killed the

Tatar warriors. He reflected, gloomily, that this did not affect his own position in any way, since he could not escape from the oasis.

Suddenly, on glancing at the crowd, Rob saw something that arrested his attention. A young girl was fastening some article to the wrist of a burly, villainous-looking Turk. The boy saw a glitter that reminded him of the traveling machine, but immediately afterward the man and the girl bent their heads over the fellow's wrist in such a way that Rob could see nothing more.

While the couple were apparently examining the strange device, Rob started to his feet and walked toward them. The crowd fell back at his approach, but the man and the girl were so interested that they did not notice him. He was still several paces away when the girl put out her finger and touched the indicator on the dial.

To Rob's horror and consternation the

The Turk rose slowly into the air, with Rob clinging
to him with desperate tenacity

big Turk began to rise slowly into the air, while a howl of fear burst from the crowd. But the boy made a mighty spring and caught the Turk by his foot, clinging to it with desperate tenacity, while they both mounted steadily upward until they were far above the city of the desert.

The big Turk screamed pitifully at first, and then actually fainted away from fright. Rob was much frightened, on his part, for he knew if his hands slipped from their hold he would fall to his death. Indeed, one hand was slipping already, so he made a frantic clutch and caught firmly hold of the Turk's baggy trousers. Then, slowly and carefully, he drew himself up and seized the leather belt that encircled the man's waist. This firm grip gave him new confidence, and he began to breathe more freely.

He now clung to the body of the Turk with both legs entwined, in the way he was accustomed to cling to a tree-trunk when he climbed after cherries at home. He had conquered his fear of falling, and took time to recover his wits and his strength.

They had now reached such a tremendous height that the city looked like a speck on the desert beneath them. Knowing he must act quickly, Rob seized the dangling left arm of the unconscious Turk and raised it until he could reach the dial of the traveling machine. He feared to unclasp the machine just then, for two reasons: if it slipped from his grasp they would both plunge downward to their death; and he was not sure the machine would work at all if in any other position than fastened to the left wrist.

Rob determined to take no chances, so he left the machine attached to the Turk and turned the indicator to zero and then to " East," for he did not wish to rejoin either his enemies the Turks or his equally undesirable friends the Tatars.

After traveling eastward a few minutes

he lost sight of the city altogether; so, still clinging to the body of the Turk, he again turned the indicator and began to descend. When, at last, they landed gently upon a rocky eminence of the Kuen-Lun mountains, the boy's strength was almost exhausted, and his limbs ached with the strain of clinging to the Turk's body.

His first act was to transfer the traveling machine to his own wrist and to see that his other electrical devices were safely bestowed in his pockets. Then he sat upon the rock to rest until the Turk recovered consciousness.

Presently the fellow moved uneasily, rolled over, and then sat up and stared at his surroundings. Perhaps he thought he had been dreaming, for he rubbed his eyes and looked again with mingled surprise and alarm. Then, seeing Rob, he uttered a savage shout and drew his dagger.

Rob smiled and pointed the electric tube

at the man, who doubtless recognized its power, for he fell back scowling and trembling.

"This place seems like a good jog from civilization," remarked the boy, as coolly as if his companion could understand what he said; "but as your legs are long and strong you may be able to find your way. It's true you're liable to starve to death, but if you do it will be your own misfortune and not my fault."

The Turk glared at him sullenly, but did not attempt to reply.

Rob took out his box of tablets, ate one of them and offered another to his enemy. The fellow accepted it ungraciously enough, but seeing Rob eat one he decided to follow his example, and consumed the tablet with a queer expression of distrust upon his face.

"Brave man!" cried Rob, laughingly; "you've avoided the pangs of starvation for a time, anyhow, so I can leave you with a clear conscience."

Without more ado he turned the indicator of the traveling machine and mounted into the air, leaving the Turk sitting upon the rocks and staring after him in comical bewilderment.

CHAPTER FIFTEEN

A BATTLE WITH MONSTERS

OUR young adventurer never experienced a more grateful feeling of relief and security than when he found himself once more high in the air, alone, and in undisputed possession of the electrical devices bestowed upon him by the Demon.

The dangers he had passed through since landing at the city of the desert and the desperate chance that alone had permitted him to regain the traveling machine made him shudder at the bare recollection and rendered him more sober and thoughtful than usual.

We who stick closely to the earth's surface can scarcely realize how Rob could travel through the air at such dizzy heights without any fear or concern whatsoever. But he had come to consider the air a veritable refuge. Experience had given him implicit confidence in the powers of the electrical instrument whose unseen forces carried him so swiftly and surely, and while the tiny, watch-like machine was clasped to his wrist he felt himself to be absolutely safe.

Having slipped away from the Turk and attained a fair altitude, he set the indicator at zero and paused long enough to consult his map and decide what direction it was best for him to take. The mischance that had swept him unwittingly over the countries of Europe had also carried him more than half way around the world from his home. Therefore the nearest way to reach America would be to continue traveling to the eastward.

So much time had been consumed at the

desert oasis that he felt he must now hasten if he wished to reach home by Saturday afternoon; so, having quickly come to a decision, he turned the indicator and began a swift flight into the east.

For several hours he traveled above the great desert of Gobi, but by noon signs of a more fertile country began to appear, and, dropping to a point nearer the earth, he was able to observe closely the country of the Chinese, with its crowded population and ancient but crude civilization.

Then he came to the Great Wall of China and to mighty Peking, above which he hovered some time, examining it curiously. He really longed to make a stop there, but with his late experiences fresh in his mind he thought it much safer to view the wonderful city from a distance.

Resuming his flight he presently came to the gulf of Laou Tong, whose fair face was freckled with many ships of many nations,

and so on to Korea, which seemed to him a
land fully a century behind the times.

Night overtook him while speeding across
the Sea of Japan, and having a great desire
to view the Mikado's famous islands, he put
the indicator at zero, and, coming to a full
stop, composed himself to sleep until morning, that he might run no chances of being
carried beyond his knowledge during the
night.

You might suppose it no easy task to
sleep suspended in mid-air, yet the magnetic currents controlled by the traveling
machine were so evenly balanced that Rob
was fully as comfortable as if reposing upon
a bed of down. He had become somewhat
accustomed to passing the night in the air
and now slept remarkably well, having no
fear of burglars or fire or other interrup-
tions that dwellers in cities are subject to.

One thing, however, he should have remembered: that he was in an ancient and

little known part of the world and reposing above a sea famous in fable as the home of many fierce and terrible creatures; while not far away lay the land of the dragon, the simurg and other ferocious monsters.

Rob may have read of these things in fairy tales and books of travel, but if so they had entirely slipped his mind; so he slumbered peacefully and actually snored a little, I believe, towards morning.

But even as the red sun peeped curiously over the horizon he was awakened by a most unusual disturbance—a succession of hoarse screams and a pounding of the air as from the quickly revolving blades of some huge windmill.

He rubbed his eyes and looked around.

Coming towards him at his right hand was an immense bird, whose body seemed almost as big as that of a horse. Its wide-open, curving beak was set with rows of pointed teeth, and the talons held against its breast and turned threateningly outward were more powerful and dreadful than a tiger's claws.

While, fascinated and horrified, he watched the approach of this feathered monster, a scream sounded just behind him and the next instant the stroke of a mighty wing sent him whirling over and over through the air.

He soon came to a stop, however, and saw that another of the monsters had come upon him from the rear and was now, with its mate, circling closely around him, while both uttered continuously their hoarse, savage cries.

Rob wondered why the Garment of Repulsion had not protected him from the blow of the bird's wing; but, as a matter of fact, it had protected him. For it was not the wing itself but the force of the eddying currents of air that had sent him whirling away from the monster. With the indicator at zero the magnetic currents and the opposing powers of attraction and repulsion were so evenly balanced that any violent atmospheric disturbance affected him in the same way that thistledown is affected by a summer breeze. He had noticed something of this before, but whenever a strong wind was blowing he was accustomed to rise to a position above the air currents. This was the first time he had slept with the indicator at zero.

The huge birds at once renewed their attack, but Rob had now recovered his wits sufficiently to draw the electric tube from his pocket. The first one to dart towards him received the powerful electric current direct from the tube, and fell stunned and fluttering to the surface of the sea, where it floated motionless. Its mate, perhaps warned by this sudden disaster, renewed its circling flight, moving so swiftly that Rob could scarcely follow it, and drawing nearer and nearer every moment to its intended victim. The boy could not turn in the air very quickly, and he feared an attack in the back, mistrusting the saving power of the Garment of Repulsion under such circumstances; so in desperation he pressed his finger upon the button of the tube and whirled the instrument around his head in the opposite direction to that in which the monster was circling. Presently the current and the bird met, and with one last scream the creature tumbled downwards to join its fellow upon the waves, where they lay like two floating islands.

Their presence had left a rank, sickening stench in the surrounding atmosphere, so Rob made haste to resume his journey and was soon moving rapidly eastward.

He could not control a shudder at the recollection of his recent combat, and realized the horror of a meeting with such creatures by one who had no protection from their sharp beaks and talons.

" It's no wonder the Japs draw ugly

pictures of those monsters," he thought. " People who live in these parts must pass most of their lives in a tremble."

The sun was now shining brilliantly, and when the beautiful islands of Japan came in sight Rob found that he had recovered his wonted cheerfulness. He moved along slowly, hovering with curious interest over the quaint and picturesque villages and watching the industrious Japanese patiently toiling at their tasks. Just before he reached Tokio he came to a military fort, and for nearly an hour watched the skilful maneuvers of a regiment of soldiers at their morning drill. They were not very big people, compared with other nations, but they seemed alert and well trained, and the boy decided it would require a brave enemy to face them on a field of battle.

Having at length satisfied his curiosity as to Japanese life and customs Rob prepared for his long flight across the Pacific Ocean.

By consulting his map he discovered that

should he maintain his course due east, as before, he would arrive at a point in America very near to San Francisco, which suited his plans excellently.

Having found that he moved more swiftly when farthest from the earth's surface, because the air was more rarefied and offered less resistance, Rob mounted upwards until the islands of Japan were mere specks visible through the clear, sunny atmosphere.

Then he began his eastward flight, the broad surface of the Pacific seeming like a blue cloud far beneath him.

CHAPTER SIXTEEN

SHIPWRECKED MARINERS

AMPLE proof of Rob's careless and restless nature having been frankly placed before the reader in these pages, you will doubtless be surprised when I relate that during the next few hours our young gentleman suffered from a severe attack of homesickness, becoming as gloomy and unhappy in its duration as ever a homesick boy could be.

It may have been because he was just then cut off from all his fellow-creatures and even from the world itself; it may have been because he was satiated with marvels and with the almost absolute control over the powers which the Demon had conferred upon him; or it may have been because he was born and reared a hearty, healthy American boy, with a disposition to battle openly with the world and take his chances equally with his fellows, rather than be placed in such an exclusive position that no one could hope successfully to oppose him.

Perhaps he himself did not know what gave him this horrible attack of "the blues," but the truth is he took out his handkerchief and cried like a baby from very loneliness and misery.

There was no one to see him, thank goodness! and the tears gave him considerable relief. He dried his eyes, made an honest struggle to regain his cheerfulness, and then muttered to himself:

"If I stay up here, like an air-bubble in the sky, I shall certainly go crazy. I suppose there's nothing but water to look at down below, but if I could only sight a ship, or even see a fish jump, it would do me no end of good."

Thereupon he descended until, as the ocean's surface came nearer and nearer, he discovered a tiny island lying almost directly underneath him. It was hardly big enough to make a dot on the biggest map, but a clump of trees grew in the central portion, while around the edges were jagged rocks protecting a sandy beach and a stretch of flower-strewn upland leading to the trees.

It looked very beautiful from Rob's elevated position, and his spirits brightened at once.

"I'll drop down and pick a bouquet," he exclaimed, and a few moments later his feet touched the firm earth of the island.

But before he could gather a dozen of the brilliant flowers a glad shout reached his ears, and, looking up, he saw two men running towards him from the trees.

They were dressed in sailor fashion, but

194

their clothing was reduced to rags and scarcely clung to their brown, skinny bodies. As they advanced they waved their arms wildly in the air and cried in joyful tones:

"A boat! a boat!"

Rob stared at them wonderingly, and had much ado to prevent the poor fellows from hugging him outright, so great was their joy at his appearance. One of them rolled upon the ground, laughing and crying by turns, while the other danced and cut capers until he became so exhausted that he sank down breathless beside his comrade.

" How came you here? " then inquired the boy, in pitying tones.

"We're shipwrecked American sailors from the bark 'Cynthia Jane,' which went down near here over a month ago," answered the smallest and thinnest of the two. " We escaped by clinging to a bit of wreckage and floated to this island, where we have nearly starved to death. Indeed, we

195

now have eaten everything on the island that was eatable, and had your boat arrived a few days later you'd have found us lying dead upon the beach!"

Rob listened to this sad tale with real sympathy.

"But I didn't come here in a boat," said he.

The men sprang to their feet with white, scared faces.

"No boat!" they cried; "are you, too, shipwrecked?"

"No;" he answered. "I flew here through the air." And then he explained to them the wonderful electric traveling machine.

But the sailors had no interest whatever in the relation. Their disappointment was something awful to witness, and one of them laid his head upon his comrade's shoulder and wept with unrestrained grief, so weak and discouraged had they become through suffering.

The disappointment of the sailors was something
awful to witness

Suddenly Rob remembered that he could assist them, and took the box of concentrated food tablets from his pocket.

" Eat these," he said, offering one to each of the sailors.

At first they could not understand that these small tablets would be able to allay the pangs of hunger; but when Rob explained their virtues the men ate them greedily. Within a few moments they were so greatly restored to strength and courage that their eyes brightened, their sunken cheeks flushed, and they were able to converse with their benefactor with calmness and intelligence.

Then the boy sat beside them upon the grass and told them the story of his acquaintance with the Demon and of all his adventures since he had come into possession of the wonderful electric contrivances. In his present mood he felt it would be a relief to confide in some one, and so these poor, lonely men were the first to hear his story.

When he related the manner in which he had clung to the Turk while both ascended into the air, the elder of the two sailors listened with rapt attention, and then, after some thought, asked:

" Why couldn't you carry one or both of us to America?"

Rob took time seriously to consider this idea, while the sailors eyed him with eager interest. Finally he said:

" I'm afraid I couldn't support your weight long enough to reach any other land. It's a long journey, and you'd pull my arms out of joint before we'd been up an hour."

Their faces fell at this, but one of them said:

" Why couldn't we swing ourselves over your shoulders with a rope? Our two bodies would balance each other and we are so thin and emaciated that we do not weigh very much.''

While considering this suggestion Rob remembered how at one time five pirates had clung to his left leg and been carried some distance through the air.

'' Have you a rope ?'' he asked.

'' No,'' was the answer; '' but there are plenty of long, tough vines growing on the island that are just as strong and pliable as ropes.''

'' Then, if you are willing to run the chances,'' decided the boy, '' I will make the attempt to save you. But I must warn you that in case I find I can not support the weight of your bodies I shall drop one or both of you into the sea.''

They looked grave at this prospect, but the biggest one said:

''We would soon meet death from starvation if you left us here on the island; so, as there is at least a chance of our being able to escape in your company I, for one, am willing to risk being drowned. It is easier and quicker than being starved. And, as I'm the heavier, I suppose you'll drop me first.''

''Certainly,'' declared Rob, promptly.

This announcement seemed to be an encouragement to the little sailor, but he said, nervously:

'' I hope you'll keep near the water, for I haven't a good head for heights—they always make me dizzy.''

''Oh, if you don't want to go,'' began Rob, '' I can easily——''

'' But I do! I do! I do! '' cried the little man, interrupting him. '' I shall die if you leave me behind! ''

'' Well, then, get your ropes, and we'll do the best we can,'' said the boy.

They ran to the trees, around the trunks of which were clinging many tendrils of greenish-brown vine which possessed remarkable strength. With their knives they cut a long section of this vine, the ends of which were then tied into loops large enough to permit the sailors to sit in them comfortably. The connecting piece Rob padded with seaweed gathered from the shore, to prevent its cutting into his shoulders.

" Now, then," he said, when all was ready, "take your places."

The sailors squatted in the loops, and Rob swung the vine over his shoulders and turned the indicator of the traveling machine to " up."

As they slowly mounted into the sky the little sailor gave a squeal of terror and clung to the boy's arm; but the other, although seemingly anxious, sat quietly in his place and made no trouble.

" D—d—don't g—g—go so high!" stammered the little one, tremblingly; "suppose we should f—f—fall!"

" Well, s'pose we should?" answered

Rob, gruffly. "You couldn't drown until you struck the water, so the higher we are the longer you'll live in case of accident."

This phase of the question seemed to comfort the frightened fellow somewhat ; but, as he said, he had not a good head for heights, and so continued to tremble in spite of his resolve to be brave.

The weight on Rob's shoulders was not so great as he had feared, the traveling machine seeming to give a certain lightness and buoyancy to everything that came into contact with its wearer.

As soon as he had reached a sufficient elevation to admit of good speed he turned the indicator once more to the east and began moving rapidly through the air, the shipwrecked sailors dangling at either side.

"This is aw—aw—awful!" gasped the little one.

"Say, you shut up !" commanded the boy, angrily. "If your friend was as big a coward as you are I'd drop you both this minute. Let go my arm and keep quiet, if you want to reach land alive.''

The fellow whimpered a little, but managed to remain silent for several minutes. Then he gave a sudden twitch and grabbed Rob's arm again.

'' S'pose—s'pose the vine should break!'' he moaned, a horrified look upon his face.

'' I've had about enough of this,'' said Rob, savagely. '' If you haven't any sense you don't deserve to live.'' He turned the indicator on the dial of the machine and they began to descend rapidly.

The little fellow screamed with fear, but Rob paid no attention to him until the feet of the two suspended sailors were actually dipping into the waves, when he brought their progress to an abrupt halt.

'' Wh—wh—what are you g—g—going to do ?'' gurgled the cowardly sailor.

'' I'm going to feed you to the sharks— unless you promise to keep your mouth shut,'' retorted the boy. '' Now, then; de-

203

cide at once! Which will it be—sharks or
silence?''

" I won't say a word—'pon my honor, I
won't!'' said the sailor, shudderingly.

"All right; remember your promise and
we'll have no further trouble,'' remarked
Rob, who had hard work to keep from
laughing at the man's abject terror.

Once more he ascended and continued
the journey, and for several hours they rode
along swiftly and silently. Rob's shoulders
were beginning to ache with the continued
tugging of the vine upon them, but the
thought that he was saving the lives of
two unfortunate fellow-creatures gave him
strength and courage to persevere.

Night was falling when they first sighted
land; a wild and seemingly uninhabited
stretch of the American coast. Rob made
no effort to select a landing place, for he
was nearly worn out with the strain and
anxiety of the journey. He dropped his
burden upon the brow of a high bluff over-

looking the sea and, casting the vine from his shoulders, fell to the earth exhausted and half fainting.

CHAPTER SEVENTEEN

THE COAST OF OREGON

WHEN he had somewhat recovered, Rob sat up and looked around him. The elder sailor was kneeling in earnest prayer, offering grateful thanks for his escape from suffering and death. The younger one lay upon the ground sobbing and still violently agitated by recollections of the frightful experiences he had undergone. Although he did not show his feelings as plainly as the men, the boy was none the less gratified at having been instrumental in saving the lives of two fellow-beings.

The darkness was by this time rapidly

enveloping them, so Rob asked his companions to gather some brushwood and light a fire, which they quickly did. The evening was cool for the time of year, and the heat from the fire was cheering and grateful; so they all lay near the glowing embers and fell fast asleep.

The sound of voices aroused Rob next morning, and on opening his eyes and gazing around he saw several rudely dressed men approaching. The two shipwrecked sailors were still sound asleep.

Rob stood up and waited for the strangers to draw near. They seemed to be fishermen, and were much surprised at finding three people asleep upon the bluff.

"Whar 'n thunder 'd ye come from?" asked the foremost fisherman, in a surprised voice.

" From the sea," replied the boy. "My friends here are shipwrecked sailors from the 'Cynthia Jane.'"

" But how'd ye make out to climb the

bluff?'' inquired a second fisherman; '' no one ever did it afore, as we knows on.''

'' Oh, that is a long story,'' replied the boy, evasively.

The two sailors had awakened and now saluted the new-comers. Soon they were exchanging a running fire of questions and answers.

'' Where are we ?'' Rob heard the little sailor ask.

'' Coast of Oregon,'' was the reply. '' We're about seven miles from Port Orford by land an' about ten miles by sea.''

'' Do you live at Port Orford?'' inquired the sailor.

'' That's what we do, friend; an' if your party wants to join us we'll do our best to make you comf'table, bein' as you're shipwrecked an' need help.''

Just then a loud laugh came from another group, where the elder sailor had been trying to explain Rob's method of flying through the air.

" Laugh all you want to," said the sailor, sullenly; " it's true—ev'ry word of it !' ''

" Mebbe you think it, friend," answered a big, good-natured fisherman; " but it's well known that shipwrecked folks go crazy sometimes, an' imagine strange things. Your mind seems clear enough in other ways, so I advise you to try and forget your dreams about flyin'."

Rob now stepped forward and shook hands with the sailors.

" I see you have found friends," he said to them, " so I will leave you and continue my journey, as I'm in something of a hurry."

Both sailors began to thank him profusely for their rescue, but he cut them short.

" That's all right. Of course I couldn't leave you on that island to starve to death, and I'm glad I was able to bring you away with me."

" But you threatened to drop me into the

sea," remarked the little sailor, in a grieved voice.

"So I did," said Rob, laughing; "but I wouldn't have done it for the world—not even to have saved my own life. Good-by!"

He turned the indicator and mounted skyward, to the unbounded amazement of the fishermen, who stared after him with round eyes and wide open mouths.

"This sight will prove to them that the sailors are not crazy," he thought, as he turned to the south and sped away from the bluff. "I suppose those simple fishermen will never forget this wonderful occurrence, and they'll probably make reg'lar heroes of the two men who have crossed the Pacific through the air."

He followed the coast line, keeping but a short distance above the earth, and after an hour's swift flight reached the city of San Francisco.

His shoulders were sore and stiff from the

heavy strain upon them of the previous day, and he wished more than once that he had some of his mother's household liniment to rub them with. Yet so great was his delight at reaching once more his native land that all discomforts were speedily forgotten.

Much as he would have enjoyed a day in the great metropolis of the Pacific slope, Rob dared not delay longer than to take a general view of the place, to note its handsome edifices and to wonder at the throng of Chinese inhabiting one section of the town.

These things were much more plainly and quickly viewed by Rob from above than by threading a way through the streets on foot; for he looked down upon the city as a bird does, and covered miles with a single glance.

Having satisfied his curiosity without attempting to alight, he turned to the southeast and followed the peninsula as far as Palo Alto, where he viewed the magnificent buildings of the university. Changing his

course to the east, he soon reached Mount
Hamilton, and, being attracted by the great
tower of the Lick Observatory, he hovered
over it until he found he had attracted the
excited gaze of its inhabitants, who doubtless observed him very plainly through the
big telescope.

But so unreal and seemingly impossible
was the sight witnessed by the learned
astronomers that they have never ventured
to make the incident public, although long
after the boy had darted away into the east
they argued together concerning the marvelous and incomprehensible vision. Afterward they secretly engrossed the circum-
stance upon their records, but resolved
never to mention it in public, lest their wisdom and veracity should be assailed by the
skeptical.

Meantime Rob rose to a higher altitude,
and sped swiftly across the great continent.
By noon he sighted Chicago, and after a
brief inspection of the place from the air

determined to devote at least an hour to forming the acquaintance of this most wonderful and cosmopolitan city.

CHAPTER EIGHTEEN

A NARROW ESCAPE

THE Auditorium Tower, where "the weather man" sits to flash his reports throughout the country, offered an inviting place for the boy to alight. He dropped quietly upon the roof of the great building and walked down the staircase until he reached the elevators, by means of which he descended to the ground floor without exciting special attention.

The eager rush and hurry of the people crowding the sidewalks impressed Rob with the idea that they were all behind time and were trying hard to catch up. He found

it impossible to walk along comfortably
without being elbowed and pushed from
side to side; so a half hour's sight-seeing
under such difficulties tired him greatly. It
was a beautiful afternoon, and finding himself upon the Lake Front, Rob hunted up
a vacant bench and sat down to rest.

Presently an elderly gentleman with a reserved and dignified appearance and dressed
in black took a seat next to the boy and
drew a magazine from his pocket. Rob saw
that he opened it to an article on "The
Progress of Modern Science," in which
he seemed greatly interested.

After a time the boy remembered that he
was hungry, not having eaten a tablet in
more than twenty-four hours. So he took
out the silver box and ate one of the small,
round disks it contained.

"What are those?" inquired the old gentleman in a soft voice. "You are too
young to be taking patent medicines."

"These are not medicines, exactly," an-

swered the boy, with a smile. "They are
Concentrated Food Tablets, stored with
nourishment by means of electricity. One
of them furnishes a person with food for an
entire day."

The old gentleman stared at Rob a moment and then laid down his magazine and
took the box in his hands, examining the
tablets curiously.

"Are these patented?" he asked.

"No," said Rob; "they are unknown
to any one but myself."

"I will give you a half million dollars
for the recipe to make them," said the gentleman.

"I fear I must refuse your offer," returned Rob, with a laugh.

"I'll make it a million," said the gentleman, coolly.

Rob shook his head.

"Money can't buy the recipe," he said;
"for I don't know it myself."

"Couldn't the tablets be chemically analyzed, and the secret discovered?" inquired the other.

"I don't know; but I'm not going to give any one the chance to try," declared the boy, firmly.

The old gentleman picked up his magazine without another word, and resumed his reading.

For amusement Rob took the Record of Events from his pocket and began looking at the scenes reflected from its polished plate.

Presently he became aware that the old gentleman was peering over his shoulder with intense interest. General Funston was just then engaged in capturing the rebel chief, Aguinaldo, and for a few moments both man and boy observed the occurrence with rapt attention. As the scene was replaced by one showing a secret tunnel of the Russian Nihilists, with the conspirators carrying dynamite to a recess underneath the palace of the Czar, the gentleman uttered a long sigh and asked:

"Will you sell that box?"

"No," answered Rob, shortly, and put it back into his pocket.

"I'll give you a million dollars to control the sale in Chicago alone," continued the gentleman, with an eager inflection in his smooth voice.

"You seem quite anxious to get rid of money," remarked Rob, carelessly. "How much are you worth?"

"Personally?"

"Yes."

"Nothing at all, young man. I am not offering you my own money. But with such inventions as you have exhibited I could easily secure millions of capital. Suppose we form a trust, and place them upon the market. We'll capitalize it for a hundred millions, and you can have a quarter of the stock—twenty-five millions. That would keep you from worrying about grocery bills."

" But I wouldn't need groceries if I had the tablets," said Rob, laughing.

" True enough! But you could take life easily and read your newspaper in comfort, without being in any hurry to get down town to business. Twenty-five millions would bring you a cozy little income, if properly invested."

" I don't see why one should read newspapers when the Record of Events shows all that is going on in the world," objected Rob.

" True, true! But what do you say to the proposition?"

" I must decline, with thanks. These inventions are not for sale."

The gentleman sighed and resumed his magazine, in which he became much absorbed.

Rob put on the Character Marking Spectacles and looked at him. The letters "E,"

"W" and "C" were plainly visible upon the composed, respectable looking brow of his companion.

"Evil, wise and cruel," reflected Rob, as he restored the spectacles to his pocket. "How easily such a man could impose upon people. To look at him one would think that butter wouldn't melt in his mouth!"

He decided to part company with this chance acquaintance and, rising from his seat, strolled leisurely up the walk. A moment later, on looking back, he discovered that the old gentleman had disappeared.

He walked down State Street to the river and back again, amused by the activity displayed in this busy section of the city. But the time he had allowed himself in Chicago had now expired, so he began looking around for some high building from the roof of which he could depart unnoticed.

This was not at all difficult, and selecting

one of many stores he ascended by an elevator to the top floor and from there mounted an iron stairway leading to the flat roof. As he climbed this stairway he found himself followed by a pleasant looking young man, who also seemed desirous of viewing the city from the roof.

Annoyed at the inopportune intrusion, Rob's first thought was to go back to the street and try another building; but, upon reflecting that the young man was not likely to remain long and he would soon be alone, he decided to wait. So he walked to the edge of the roof and appeared to be interested in the scenery spread out below him.

" Fine view from here, ain't it?" said the young man, coming up to him and placing his hand carelessly upon the boy's shoulder.

" It is, indeed," replied Rob, leaning over the edge to look into the street.

As he spoke he felt himself gently but firmly pushed from behind and, losing his balance, he plunged headforemost from the roof and whirled through the intervening space toward the sidewalk far below.

Terrified though he was by the sudden disaster, the boy had still wit enough remaining to reach out his right hand and move the indicator of the machine upon his left wrist to the zero mark. Immediately he paused in his fearful flight and presently came to a stop at a distance of less than fifteen feet from the flagstones which had threatened to crush out his life.

As he stared downward, trying to recover his self-possession, he saw the old gentleman he had met on the Lake Front standing just below and looking at him with a half frightened, half curious expression in his eyes.

At once Rob saw through the whole plot to kill him and thus secure possession of his electrical devices. The young man upon the roof who had attempted to push him to his death was a confederate of the innocent

222

appearing old gentleman, it seemed, and the latter had calmly awaited his fall to the pavement to seize the coveted treasures from his dead body. It was an awful idea, and Rob was more frightened than he had ever been before in his life—or ever has been since.

But now the shouts of a vast concourse of amazed spectators reached the boy's ears. He remembered that he was suspended in mid-air over the crowded street of a great city, while thousands of wondering eyes were fixed upon him.

So he quickly set the indicator to the word "up," and mounted sky-ward until the watchers below could scarcely see him. Then he fled away into the east, even yet shuddering with the horror of his recent escape from death and filled with disgust at the knowledge that there were people who held human life so lightly that they were willing to destroy it to further their own selfish ends.

"And the Demon wants such people as these to possess his electrical devices, which are as powerful to accomplish evil when in wrong hands as they are good!" thought the boy, resentfully. "This would be a fine world if Electric Tubes and Records of Events and Traveling Machines could be acquired by selfish and unprincipled persons!"

So unnerved was Rob by his recent experiences that he determined to make no more stops. However, he alighted at nightfall in the country, and slept upon the sweet hay in a farmer's barn.

But, early the next morning, before any one else was astir, he resumed his journey, and at precisely ten o'clock of this day, which was Saturday, he completed his flying trip around the world by alighting unobserved upon the well-trimmed lawn of his own home.

CHAPTER NINETEEN

ROB MAKES A RESOLUTION

WHEN Rob opened the front door he came face to face with Nell, who gave an exclamation of joy and threw herself into his arms.

"Oh, Rob!" she cried, "I'm so glad you've come. We have all been dreadfully worried about you, and mother—"

"Well, what about mother?" inquired the boy, anxiously, as she paused.

"She's been very ill, Rob; and the doctor said to-day that unless we heard from you soon he would not be able to save her life. The uncertainty about you is killing her."

Rob stood stock still, all the eager joy of his return frozen into horror at the thought that he had caused his dear mother so much suffering.

" Where is she, Nell?" he asked, brokenly.

" In her room. Come; I'll take you to her."

Rob followed with beating heart, and soon was clasped close to his mother's breast.

" Oh, my boy—my dear boy!" she murmured, and then for very joy and love she was unable to say more, but held him tight and stroked his hair gently and kissed him again and again.

Rob said little, except to promise that he would never again leave home without her full consent and knowledge. But in his mind he contrasted the love and comfort that now surrounded him with the lonely and unnatural life he had been leading and, boy though he was in years, a mighty resolution that would have been creditable to an experienced man took firm root in his heart.

He was obliged to recount all his adventures to his mother and, although he made light of the dangers he had passed through, the story drew many sighs and shudders from her.

When luncheon time arrived he met his father, and Mr. Joslyn took occasion to reprove his son in strong language for running away from home and leaving them filled with anxiety as to his fate. However, when he saw how happy and improved in health his dear wife was at her boy's return, and when he had listened to Rob's manly confession of error and expressions of repentance, he speedily forgave the culprit and treated him as genially as ever.

Of course the whole story had to be repeated, his sisters listening this time with open eyes and ears and admiring their adventurous brother immensely. Even Mr. Joslyn could not help becoming profoundly interested, but he took care not to show any pride he might feel in his son's achievements.

When his father returned to his office Rob went to his own bed-chamber and sat for a long time by the window in deep thought. When at last he aroused himself, he found it was nearly four o'clock.

"The Demon will be here presently," he said, with a thrill of aversion, "and I must be in the workshop to receive him."

Silently he stole to the foot of the attic stairs and then paused to listen. The house seemed very quiet, but he could hear his mother's voice softly humming a cradle-song that she had sung to him when he was a baby.

He had been nervous and unsettled and a little fearful until then, but perhaps the

sound of his mother's voice gave him courage, for he boldly ascended the stairs and
entered the workshop, closing and locking
the door behind him.

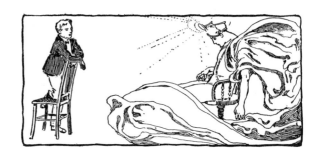

CHAPTER TWENTY

THE UNHAPPY FATE OF THE DEMON

AGAIN the atmosphere quickened and pulsed with accumulating vibrations. Again the boy found himself aroused to eager expectancy. There was a whirl in the air; a crackling like distant musketry; a flash of dazzling light—and the Demon stood before him for the third time.

" I give you greetings! " said he, in a voice not unkindly.

"Good afternoon, Mr. Demon," answered the boy, bowing gravely.

" I see you have returned safely from your trip," continued the Apparition, cheerfully, "although at one time I thought you would be unable to escape. Indeed, unless I had knocked that tube from the rascally Turk's hand as he clambered to the top of the wall, I believe you would have been at the Yarkand oasis yet—either dead or alive, as chance might determine."

"Were you there?" asked Rob.

"To be sure. And I recovered the tube for you, without which you would have been helpless. But that is the only time I saw fit to interfere in any way."

"I'm afraid I did not get a chance to give many hints to inventors or scientists," said Rob.

"True, and I have deeply regretted it," replied the Demon. "But your unusual powers caused more astonishment and consternation than you, perhaps, imagined; for many saw you whom you were too busy to notice. As a result several able electricians are now thinking new thoughts along new lines, and some of them may soon give these or similar inventions to the world."

"You are satisfied, then?" asked Rob.

"As to that," returned the Demon, composedly, "I am not. But I have hopes that with the addition of the three marvelous devices I shall present you with to-day you will succeed in arousing so much popular interest in electrical inventions as to render me wholly satisfied with the result of this experiment."

Rob regarded the brilliant apparition with a solemn face, but made no answer.

"No living person," continued the Demon, "has ever before been favored with such comforting devices for the preservation and extension of human life as yourself. You seem quite unappreciative, it is true; but since our connection I have come to realize that you are but an ordinary boy, with many boyish limitations; so I do not condemn your foolish actions too harshly."

" That is kind of you," said Rob.

" To prove my friendliness," pursued the Demon, " I have brought, as the first of to-day's offerings, this Electro-Magnetic Restorer. You see it is shaped like a thin metal band, and is to be worn upon the brow, clasping at the back of the head. Its virtues surpass those of either the fabulous 'Fountain of Youth,' or the 'Elixir of Life,' so vainly sought for in past ages. For its wearer will instantly become free from any bodily disease or pain and will enjoy perfect health and vigor. In truth, so great are its powers that even the dead may be restored to life, provided the blood has not yet chilled. In presenting you with this appliance, I feel I am bestowing upon you the greatest blessing and most longed-for boon ever bequeathed to suffering humanity."

Here he held the slender, dull-colored metallic band toward the boy.

"Keep it," said Rob.

The Demon started, and gave him an odd look.

"What did you say?" he asked.

"I told you to keep it," answered Rob. "I don't want it."

The Demon staggered back as if he had been struck.

"Don't want it!" he gasped.

"No; I've had enough of your infernal inventions!" cried the boy, with sudden anger.

He unclasped the traveling machine from his wrist and laid it on the table beside the Demon.

"There's the thing that's responsible for most of my troubles," said he, bitterly. "What right has one person to fly through the air while all his fellow-creatures crawl over the earth's surface? And why should I be cut off from all the rest of the world because you have given me this confounded traveling machine? I didn't ask for it, and

234

I won't keep it a moment longer. Give it to some one you hate more than you do me!"

The Demon stared aghast and turned his glittering eyes wonderingly from Rob to the traveling machine and back again, as if to be sure he had heard and seen aright.

"And here are your food tablets," continued the boy, placing the box upon the table. "I've only enjoyed one square meal since you gave them to me. They're all right to preserve life, of course, and answer the purpose for which they were made; but I don't believe nature ever intended us to exist upon such things, or we wouldn't have the sense of taste, which enables us to enjoy natural food. As long as I'm a human being I'm going to eat like a human being, so I've consumed my last Electrical Concentrated Food Tablet—and don't you forget it!"

The Demon sank into a chair, nerveless and limp, but still staring fearfully at the boy.

"And there's another of your unnatural devices," said Rob, putting the Automatic Record of Events upon the table beside the other things. " What right have you to capture vibrations that radiate from private and secret actions and discover them to others who have no business to know them? This would be a fine world if every body could peep into every one else's affairs, wouldn't it? And here is your Character Marker. Nice thing for a decent person to own, isn't it? Any one who would take advantage of such a sneaking invention as that would be worse than a thief! Oh, I've used them, of course, and I ought to be spanked for having been so mean and underhanded; but I'll never be guilty of looking through them again."

The Demon's face was frowning and indignant. He made a motion to rise, but thought better of it and sank back in his chair.

"As for the Garment of Protection," resumed the boy, after a pause, " I've worn
it for the last time, and here it is, at your
service. I'll put the Electric Tube with it.
Not that these are such very bad things in
themselves, but I'll have none of your magical contrivances. I'll say this, however: if
all armies were equipped with Electrical
Tubes instead of guns and swords the world
would be spared a lot of misery and unnecessary bloodshed. Perhaps they will be,
in time; but that time hasn't arrived yet."

" You might have hastened it," said the
Demon, sternly, " if you had been wise
enough to use your powers properly."

" That's just it," answered Rob. " I'm
not wise enough. Nor is the majority of
mankind wise enough to use such inventions as yours unselfishly and for the good
of the world. If people were better, and
every one had an equal show, it would be
different."

For some moments the Demon sat quietly thinking. Finally the frown left his face and he said, with animation:

"I have other inventions, which you may use without any such qualms of conscience. The Electro-Magnetic Restorer I offered you would be a great boon to your race, and could not possibly do harm. And, besides this, I have brought you what I call the Illimitable Communicator. It is a simple electric device which will enable you, wherever you may be, to converse with people in any part of the world, without the use of such crude connections as wires. In fact, you may"—

"Stop!" cried Rob. "It is useless for you to describe it, because I'll have nothing more to do with you or your inventions. I have given them a fair trial, and they've got me into all sorts of trouble and made all my friends miserable. If I was some high-up scientist it would be different; but I'm just a common boy, and I don't want to be anything else."

"But, your duty—" began the Demon.

"My duty I owe to myself and to my family," interrupted Rob. "I have never cultivated science, more than to fool with some simple electrical experiments, so I owe nothing to either science or the Demon of Electricity, so far as I can see."

"But consider," remonstrated the Demon, rising to his feet and speaking in a pleading voice, "consider the years that must elapse before any one else is likely to strike the Master Key! And, in the meanwhile, consider my helpless position, cut off from all interest in the world while I have such wonderful inventions on my hands for the benefit of mankind. If you have no love for science or for the advancement of civilization, *do* have some consideration for your fellow-creatures, and for me!"

" If my fellow-creatures would have as much trouble with your electrical inventions as I had, I am doing them a service by depriving them of your devices," said the boy. "As for yourself, I've no fault to find with you, personally. You're a very decent sort of Demon, and I've no doubt you mean well; but there's something wrong about our present combination, I'm sure. It isn't natural."

The Demon made a gesture of despair.

" Why, oh why did not some intelligent person strike the Master Key!" he moaned.

" That's it!" exclaimed Rob. " I believe that's the root of the whole evil."

" What is ?" inquired the Demon, stupidly.

" The fact that an intelligent person did not strike the Master Key. You don't seem to understand. Well, I'll explain. You're the Demon of Electricity, aren't you?"

" I am," said the other, drawing himself up proudly.

"Your mission is to obey the commands of whoever is able to strike the Master Key of Electricity."

"That is true."

"I once read in a book that all things are regulated by exact laws of nature. If that is so you probably owe your existence to those laws." The Demon nodded. "Doubtless it was intended that when mankind became intelligent enough and advanced enough to strike the Master Key, you and all your devices would not only be necessary and acceptable to them, but the world would be prepared for their general use. That seems reasonable, doesn't it?"

"Perhaps so. Yes; it seems reasonable," answered the Demon, thoughtfully.

"Accidents are always liable to happen," continued the boy. "By accident the Master Key was struck long before the world of science was ready for it—or for you. Instead of considering it an accident and paying no attention to it you immediately appeared to me—a mere boy—and offered your services."

"I was very anxious to do something," returned the Demon, evasively. "You've no idea how stupid it is for me to live invisible and unknown, while all the time I have in my possession secrets of untold benefit to the world."

"Well, you'll have to keep cool and bide your time," said Rob. "The world wasn't made in a minute, and while civilization is going on at a pretty good pace, we're not up to the Demon of Electricity yet."

"What shall I do!" groaned the Apparition, wringing his hands miserably; "oh, what shall I do!"

"Go home and lie down," replied Rob, sympathetically. "Take it easy and don't get rattled. Nothing was ever created without a use, they say; so your turn will come some day, sure! I'm sorry for you, old fellow, but it's all your own fault."

"You are right!" exclaimed the Demon,

striding up and down the room, and caus-
ing thereby such a crackling of electricity in
the air that Rob's hair became rigid enough
to stand on end. "You are right, and I
must wait—wait—wait—patiently and silently—until my bonds are loosed by intelligence rather than chance! It is a dreary
fate. But I must wait—I must wait—I
must wait!"

"I'm glad you've come to your senses,"
remarked Rob, drily. "So, if you've nothing more to say—"

"No! I have nothing more to say. There
is nothing more to say. You and I are
two. We should never have met!" retorted the Demon, showing great excitement.

"Oh, I didn't seek your acquaintance,"
said Rob. "But I've tried to treat you de-
cently, and I've no fault to find with you
except that you forgot you were a slave and
tried to be a master."

The Demon did not reply. He was bus-

243

ily forcing the various electrical devices that Rob had relinquished into the pockets of his fiery jacket.

Finally he turned with an abrupt movement.

"Good-by!" he cried. "When mortal eyes next behold me they will be those of one fit to command my services! As for you, your days will be passed in obscurity and your name be unknown to fame. Goodby,—forever!"

The room filled with a flash of white light so like a sheet of lightning that the boy went reeling backwards, half stunned and blinded by its dazzling intensity.

When he recovered himself the Demon of Electricity had disappeared.

*   *   *   *   *

Rob's heart was very light as he left the workshop and made his way down the attic stairs.

"Some people might think I was a fool to give up those electrical inventions," he reflected; "but I'm one of those persons who know when they've had enough. It strikes me the fool is the fellow who can't learn a lesson. I've learned mine, all right. It's no fun being a century ahead of the times!"

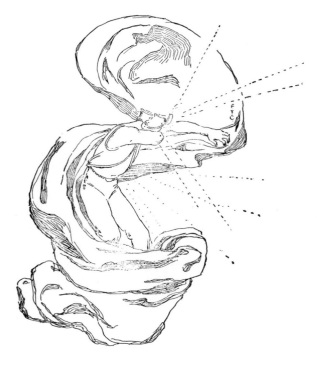